The Versus Anthology

The Versus Anthology

VS.

Edited by Josh Woods

Press 53
Winston-Salem, NC

Press 53
PO Box 30314
Winston-Salem, NC 27130

First Edition

While some stories are based on historical incidents, the situations themselves are products of the authors' imaginations. Any resemblances to actual events, places or persons, living or dead, are meant to be resemblances and not actual representations of events, places or persons.

Copyright © 2009 by Josh Woods

All rights reserved, including the right of reproduction in whole or in part in any form. For permission, contact author at editor@press53.com, or at the address above.

Cover design by Josh Woods & Kevin Watson

"Orgo VS. The Flatlanders" by Pinckney Benedict, copyright © 2009 by Pinckney Benedict, first appeared in the 2009 *Idaho Review*.

"Emile Griffith and Muhammad Ali Inhabit the Bodies of the Last Roosters to Legally Fight in Louisiana, August 15, 2008 & Peleas de Gallo: Hector Velazquez, 32, Caesar Julius's Cocker, Pumpkin Center, LA, August 15, 2008" by Michael Garriga, copyright © 2009 by Michael Garriga, first appeared in the 2009 *Louisiana Literature* under the title "In the Gallodrome" and "Peleas de Gallo."

"The Impossible Division by Zero: Hulk VS. Hel, Goddess of the Underworld" by Okla Elliott, copyright © 2009 by Okla Elliott, first appeared in *The Indiana Review*.

"The Girl I Thought I Would Marry When I Was Six VS. The Woman I Did Marry When I Was Twenty-Six" by Michael Kimball, copyright © 2009 by Michael Kimball, first appeared in *Dear Everybody*.

Printed on acid-free paper.

ISBN 978-0-9824416-1-9

Contents

INTRODUCTION		vii
My Father VS. The Soap Lady	*Alexander Lumans*	1
The Six Million Dollar Man VS. Jaws	*Brad Vice*	9
Orgo VS. The Flatlanders	*Pinckney Benedict*	15
The Devil's Advocate: Moe Howard VS. Mother Teresa	*John McNally*	49
Emile Griffith and Muhammad Ali Inhabit the Bodies of the Last Roosters to Legally Fight in Louisiana, August 15, 2008 & Peleas de Gallo: Hector Velazquez, 32, Caesar Julius's Cocker, Pumpkin Center, LA, August 15, 2008	*Michael Garriga*	59
Wrestling with Andy Kaufman	*Margaret McMullan*	63
The 103rd Story, or How Murph Jr. Beats Murph to the Top of the Sears Tower	*John Flaherty*	73
Theodore Roosevelt VS. Spring Heeled Jack, an Interviewings by Me, El Pollo Diablo, Dead Pirate of the Netherworld	*El Pollo Diablo*	79
Dragonfruit VS. Dragonfruit: The Versus & The Verdict	*Matt Guenette & Michael Theune*	87

Amy VS. Herself	*Danielle Girard Kraus*	91
Kyle Minor VS. Else Richter	*Kyle Minor & Joshua Archer*	97
Amelia Earhart VS. The 'Burbs	*Susan Woodring*	113
The Dark Saint	*Curtis Smith*	123
Arthur Miller Walks into a Bar, A Five Minute Screenplay: Arthur Miller VS. Joe DiMaggio	*Andrew Scott*	125
The Girl I Thought I Would Marry When I Was Six VS. The Woman I Did Marry When I Was Twenty-Six	*Michael Kimball*	133
The Impossible Division by Zero: Hulk VS. Hel, Goddess of the Underworld	*Okla Elliott*	135
Barbie VS. Stalin	*Stacey Richter*	147
Lynch VS. Dali	*John Dimes*	152
Love VS. Lust	*Laura Benedict*	155
Dorothy Gale VS. Alice Liddell	*Becky Hagenston*	159
Fighting Bull	*K. H. Solomon*	163
Jesus VS. Thor	*Josh Woods*	165
CONTRIBUTOR BIOGRAPHIES		173

Introduction

Let's pick a fight. And not just any fight, let's pick a fight between our most iconic characters and forces, or even between extraordinary, original characters, or with people from our very real pasts. Anything goes. Some of today's most innovative writers and artists did just that in this book: each picked a conflict, made it come to life, and now present the aftermath to you here in the first anthology to take up this challenge, *Versus*.

Versus showcases wild, fun, and stirring works of short fiction, poetry, creative non-fiction, screenplay, flash, epistolary, duel, experimental, and even comic/graphic narrative, all built on theme of pitting one against another, a formula as simple as "____ VS. ____." Find out what happens when we put our pop icons up against religious icons, when characters from classic literature battle it out alongside dictators from real history, when monsters and heroines, beasts and heroes, artists and athletes, fathers and sons, poultry and presidents, comedians and saints all contend in their equally powerful but absolutely unique ways. Witness everything from intimate struggle of everyday folk to epic apocalypse of gods and kings. Whether you have a taste for the bold or the subtle, the humorous or the poignant, the surreal or the unbelievably real, you'll find it here.

Despite the fact that this is the very first *Versus* anthology, the concept behind this collection is really nothing new. I have played this versus thought-game with my friends, as has nearly everyone I know, since childhood—we would build tales and argue for hours about who would win in a fight between He-Man and Conan, or about the infinitely cunning MacGyver VS. Cyclops from X-Men; I would even play out versus scenarios alone between my incompatible action figures, like a towering Thundercat VS. a petite '80s G.I. Joe—yet we were less-than-knowingly participating in a tradition as old as storytelling itself. The ancient Greeks, who clearly understood the value and power of this concept, allow us now to articulate it as the *agon*—the central conflict in a work of literature, the struggle for the foremost place. The agon of Achilles and Hector, the agon of Odysseus and the Cyclops Polyphemus, even Odysseus' more incompatible struggle, the agon of him and Calypso—these and countless other instances of the agon form the deepest foundations of our literature and art as we know it. And if our culture has come about through an ancestral marriage between Athens and Jerusalem, as many say, then we can go to the Bible—either Hebrew or Christian—and find as many shining examples of the agon as we care to. But, again, even these ancient examples participate in a tradition older than themselves. The oldest story I can find still on sale in the bookstore is *The Epic of Gilgamesh*, and if that isn't driven by the agon—chock full of versus moments—I don't know what is.

That, of course, is to say nothing of the equally deep and rich traditions of the agon in the varied Eastern literatures, the myriad independent indigenous literatures, and the many other non-Western worlds of storytelling. In fact, non-Western traditions often display much greater self-awareness and unapologetic exuberance in the natural longing for the agon.

Because of all this, the revitalization of graphic narrative in our recent culture ought to be no real surprise. (I say *revitalization* only in the long-view sense—graphic narrative is gaining more power now than it ever has in America, but people have been recording stories with series of pictures longer than we have with letters. Our very letters themselves are nothing more than pictograms corrupted and altered across ages and civilizations. Just flip your "A" upside-down—see a bull?) Graphic narratives, or comics, are the agon boldly pronounced, and we like that; people like that. Our most popular movies are the agon boldly, from comic-gone-film and folktale-gone-film (a la Zack Snyder, Guillermo Del Toro, etc., etc.) to film-gone-film (a la Quentin Tarentino, etc.). Likewise, our dawning age of videogame/simulation is driven more so by the agon than by any other of its meritorious qualities (experiential, educational, empathetic, communal, etc.); Midwestern grade-school children this very week know what it was like to be a peasant soldier conscripted into waiting in the snow for German forces at Stalingrad and holding a malfunctioning rifle alongside dear friends, better than any post WWII generation ever has at that age, and they know it because they simply wanted to boot up a videogame and battle it out against badguys in tanks.

We have never really lost our taste for the agon, for a versus-style narrative. However (and quite oddly), I do notice a trend in the literary community, a trend which seems to stretch back only a half-century or so, to regard such explicit versus-style conflict, or at least an explicitly stated intention of versus-style conflict, as nothing more than a form of play, as something not to be taken seriously. This is worth teasing out, I think. The idea of versus as "play" I will happily concede; the "not to be taken seriously" part I must respectfully turn against itself. If nothing else, let this anthology be an exhibition of serious play.

In the case of creating literature and art, I prefer serious play to mean taking an intriguing or outrageous concept much too sincerely, and then continuing it at much too great an extent. Too seriously, too far. I think the only way we can attain that bizarre "too" quality in "too seriously, too far" is to be certain that it is the play that we take seriously, the indulging in and enjoying of the production and the product. Once we begin taking ourselves seriously, or our narrative authority seriously, or our audiences seriously, or our critics seriously, or our agendas seriously, well, then we've lost it—we've broken away from that mode which has helped to produce some of the greatest and most enjoyable works in history. And as educators Botturi and Loh point out, *play* most certainly is a mode—not an activity opposite of *work*, as *leisure* is, but a mode of human experience that can encompass leisure activities as easily as it can work activities (Botturi & Loh; 2008, in press, publisher Springer, ed. Miller, *Games: Purpose and Potential in Eduication*). Especially when it comes to writing and art, working in the mode of play—serious play—produces very real results.

Most importantly, as readers, serious play engages us in powerful ways that we often can't pinpoint, something that moves beyond technique and rhetorical/artistic skill—maybe we'll say certain authors or their works have tuned themselves to some charismatic frequency, or maybe we'll simply say we like them, that's it, and devil take the explanations. Either way, these works satisfy some hungry part of our imaginations, whether that hunger existed beforehand or emerged from the work itself. In other words, works of serious play are simply enjoyable.

I must contend (since this book is the best place to pick a fight) that those who disagree with what I've said here, as correct as they might possibly prove to be, are necessarily setting up a telling scenario: themselves VS. *Versus*. We cannot avoid it; the agon contains us. And I turned critique back on itself again—bwahahaha!

But really, turning things back against themselves takes us directly to the word itself, *versus*, which originates from the Latin for "to turn against," which comes from a similar "turn or bend" meaning out of an earlier Indo-Euro family of words, forming shared roots with the word *verse*. It's easy to envision how the end of a line of poetry turns back and begins anew at the next line, thus earning the name *verse*, and this vision is the ur-vision of versus. A specifically "versus" piece of writing or art ought to somehow turn—on itself, on the reader, on something—so that what it once was has changed and is no more, its end becoming a new beginning. I'm delighted that each of the works you'll find here, from the adventurous to the traditional, from satirical to passionate, from reflective to wild, is a true versus piece.

Perhaps you're prepared enough, perhaps I'm training you too hard, perhaps I just need to tug the gloves on you, push you into the ring, and let you start swinging on your own. So be it. Start turning those pages and go pick the fight of your life.

Josh Woods
Carbondale, IL
April 2009

The Versus Anthology

VS.

Alexander Lumans

My Father VS. the Soap Lady

Both my father and the soap lady have only their right arms. The soap lady willingly gave hers up as a gift to a boy in town named Rollo who is now dead without clear reason; my father was not so intentional in his loss. His left arm was pulled from his body in that war in Vietnam, back before I was born, and his friends in the jungle could not find the arm to reattach it. To this day, my father believes it was his own company's artillery shell that did the job. He's still bitter. Most mornings, I see him bite his tongue and close his eyes when the phantom pain comes and I think about how strange he'd look with two arms. He's told me, over and over, that ever since the soap lady rose from our town's lake three years ago, he's not gone a day without those phantom nails dragging between his absent fingertips and the beginning of his stump just above the elbow. We say she's a lady because we don't know better. Everyone just steers clear of her. My father does this too because he wants to avoid looking weak; he cares about what I think of him, missing parts or not. It's not like he's not told me this. But I see it in his right arm when he guides me up to bed, firmly, but also with some hesitation when he goes in for the goodnight hug. Even with his hesitation, there are times when I am close enough to him that I know what he's thinking and feeling and I want to be able to use words like him and hate the soap lady, like him. The night after the boy named Rollo is pronounced dead, my father's hug is long and shaky and he says I don't have to take a bath, but I do have to lock the windows.

Three days later, a week after my fourteenth birthday, September, my father is angrier than I've ever seen him. He and I are walking through the woods to the town lake. My father is over six feet tall in his canvas shorts and bright red flannel shirt and big old Wolverine boots. He always leans to the left a little as if he's off balance, like when he's hunkered down over a soldering iron and welding pick or when he's propped up against a kitchen counter, pretending to look at his watch that isn't there. His black hair is always the same: stiff and short and bristly. And he's bigger around in the shoulders than his waist, which is good because he can carry me upside-down across the lawn and toss me into a leaf pile without losing his breath. He's like a big whisker-less catfish, all squints and bulk and cool skin. I'm sure he could break bones with that one hand, and not because he's got major muscles—I think it's more because he knows pressure points. He's smart like that. He's almost a big me; a big me that I don't think I am yet. But he can also be this huge, angry, impulsive man—one that I am not so sure I want to become. Sometimes, his anger is so much, it's like a fire in the room, and I am sweating.

On our way to the lake, I'm carrying his short lathing hatchet, the handle bound up in leather trim, the head wrapped in an oilcloth, the blade sharpened on a whetstone for three mornings in a row. My father holds my free hand high and his fingers are warm and dry and I'm not used to this kind of touch. He breathes through his nose and trips on pine roots and keeps marching on and I can only think of Rollo and his closed casket.

The lake is as large as my middle school grounds and shaped like a donkey's head—I've been here before, without his permission, to see if what all the other kids say is true: that you can toss a Coke can or coffee mug or candle saucer into the water and it will show up on the shore in less than a minute. Something about how the soap lady wants to keep her lake clean. How she can feel everything inside her lake. This means the shore is crammed full of slashed tractor tires, long chrome motorcycle mufflers, detergent bottles with the poison stickers and laundry baskets full of diapers; everything we want to get rid of. I don't tell my father I know where the lake is because then he'll know I've been here and all that anger will turn on me.

We get to the lake and I'm not surprised that the water is perfectly flat. No one comes to swim or take out paddleboats anymore. This is dark water, darker than I remember. It looks more like oil than something drinkable. Already I don't like being here. The hatchet feels heavier. There's something terrible in the way there's no sound around, not even a couple birds in the short spiky bushes and crepe myrtles that crowd the shoreline. My father takes the hatchet from me and points to the nearest patch of these azalea bushes and I know he wants me to stay there. He doesn't even say anything, he's that focused. I hide among the leaves but stick my head out and watch and wait and wonder if he's as scared as I am.

My father stands at the water's edge. Then he takes two steps forward in his big clompers. Before he takes a third, the water churns and bubbles fifteen feet out. It looks like someone dropped in a string of firecrackers. I want to duck down, but I don't.

Out of the white foam, four thin, white, tiny tips rise up. They are fingers. Four fingers. Then a half-globe beside them. A forehead. My father is trembling, concentrating, leaning forward. More of the fingers, so long and narrow, and that face, spongy-looking and maggot-pale. No nose, only an O-shaped mouth with white lips and black tongue. There's no real face in hers. Just features. And those eyes. It is more like her eyes are holes cut through her head, and you can see the black lake behind her. The Soap Lady. The water slicks from her soap skin as quick as down the back of a duck. And it's true: she has no left arm. It's gone at the shoulder, not even a stump. Her stomach sticks out like she's not eaten for months, as if all that soap inside her is just boiling and bubbling up and pushing outward with smoke. Only her feet stay under.

There they stand, my father and the soap lady, strange mirrors of each other. Here is where I lend my father my strength; here is where we are most family.

My father slides the oilcloth off the axehead and hefts the weapon once, then lets it fall naturally in his hand as he gauges the two pounds. He brings the hammerhead up against his shoulder and makes to yell, but she catches him first:

She says, "You are like me." Her voice is a mixture of spring hail on the roof and old, creaky porch swing ropes. It sounds all around the lake. But her words are not the worst part. It's that her mouth does not move when she speaks.

My father yells back, "I am not a monster!"

She says, "You are like me, and I can make you like me."

"Nothing good and holy looks anything like you."

"It does."

"You killed that boy—Rollo," he says. "What did you do to him?"

"I helped him clean. He needed help."

"You're lying: he's dead."

"I know."

"You're nothing." My father points the hatchet toward her.

She says, "We all make mistakes." Her left shoulder twitches, like a tooth ready to break free of the gum.

Without another word, my father strikes out into the water, hatchet raised, ready to haul off and throw. The water surface reaches his shins, his knees, his belly, soaking his clothes and filling his boots until he stops—any further and he'll go in over his head, even though the soap lady is still standing with only her feet underwater. The cold is much worse; it's painful and it squeezes hard. He keeps the hatchet high above the water as if it might dissolve like sugar.

Then the soap lady takes off running—not straight at my father, but rather in a wide circle, coming around on his left, and all this on the water like it was made of vinyl. He tracks her, finding it difficult to move in the brackish water.

The soap lady charges toward him and leaps to his left when she gets close. He swings the hatchet across his chest and hits nothing. She gets close enough in the parrying dive that her hand brushes the stump of his left arm and he nearly drops the weapon: her touch is a hot, wicked one. He's all shakes and nerves now. Where those long, dreadful fingers ran along his bicep, the flannel has turned shock white in four brilliant streaks.

He whips around to chase her. She runs and skips across the lake surface, mocking him, now thirty feet away, so nimble; those strides are perfect and graceful and her soap feet slap hard on the water. She turns toward him again, coming from the opposite direction, and charges with no expression but that skullish face. My father plants his left foot forward, angles his left shoulder in front, and brings the hatchet back behind his head. He lines up a clear shot in front. Again, she leaps early and to his left, clears his hatchet swing, and slides away on the watertop. And again, she catches his stump with her burning fingers. When he looks at his arm, the flannel sleeve dissolves away white.

He believes in a pattern: she will go out in a wide arc, then drive forward and skate off to the left a few feet before him and she will reach for his arm a third time. At the point of leaping he will catch her. He is all over her plan.

The soap lady skirts swiftly across the water and comes in fast from a third direction. He readies the hatchet. He mock swipes once. And when she is eight feet from him, he chucks the weapon straight at her blown-up belly and the weapon goes sailing end over end, a perfect blur of wood and iron, dead on in its aim. But the soap lady is even quicker. She dodges to the right this time, slipping easily by the hatchet, and lunges out of my father's periphery while the axehead slices into the black water. He is furious at the easy trick. Then the hissing sound comes again and the slapping of feet right behind him and the soap lady's hand is suddenly gripping his stump.

Her fingers wrap all the way around his arm and burn away the layers of skin. He cannot pull his weaker limb out of her hand, no matter how hard he jolts back and forth. His shout is louder than baseballs hitting a wooden backstop, but the words don't make sense. He looks up into those shark-black eyes and slams his fist into her flat face with an awkwardly aimed but still strong right cross. This breaks her hold and knocks her away onto the lake where she curls up and covers her smashed face and hole-eyes and ghastly mouth, and where her threaded fingers don't cover, there's a distinct imprint of his knuckles in her cheek that felt like cooked steak when he hit it. He would strike a pose like he did in his pictures from the jungle war, but it'd all be underwater.

When he takes a scouting glance there's no trace of the soap lady. The greasy lake is a dead zone. My father charges toward shore, pumping his knees high to plow through the murk, favoring his left side. He regrets twice-over having given up his advantage on a loose toss; he can't even pinpoint where to start looking for the hatchet.

Before he clears the water her voice comes back, harsher: "You should always clean your mistakes, too." He whirls around.

Where he was seconds ago now stands the soap lady, rising from the depths. Her lithe waist, her thighs, her knees that look like bowls of curdled milk. The burnt smell of a dirty fire hits him. It's his own arm that reeks and he shakes it up and down as if it is something to put out.

The soap lady is changing. She crouches down, she vibrates, she froths at the mouth. The way she's concentrating so hard, like my father had been when she first appeared, she could burst into a million bits of soap and cover the world in her clean debris. But instead, something grows from nothing. First a thin, silvery string, tiny enough to lose in the wind, snakes out of her shoulder like one long phantom-vein. Then it widens, bulges in places. The string becomes a rope, becomes a sheetline, becomes white fruit hung from a clothesline. These are muscles, it's true. The biceps form, the elbow sharpens, the forearm hardens into mashed lumps. The wrist puffs up like a ring of marshmallows and the fingers burst out from a palm you could draw a picture on, it's so flat and white. The new arm is perfect. The new arm is her arm. The fight is her win.

And all this while, my father's arm throbs and feels like it will split open. He drops to his knees in the shallows and doesn't turn away from the wound. Instead, he watches in horror as a feathery slip of quicksilver pours out the end of his stump and blows up like a balloon and hardens into an arm—an arm made entirely of soap—and his new fingers touch the greasy lake. He bites his collar to keep from shouting. It's all so quick to him, but there it is. The arm. He wants to tear it off. This new arm that is not his. Yet the instinct to turn it, clench it, twist it, flail it into the sky, is alive inside him.

My father gets down on one knee. He slips his soap arm into the water, finds no resistance. At once, the entire lake is at his fingertips, every miniscule drop and depth, the whole shoreline within reach. It's an invigorating thing.

That's when he notices the hatchet sliding up the lakebed toward him, or feels it, rather, senses it drawn up into the shallows. The hardness of that wood and metal and a strange heat inside. My father grabs the hatchet's helve, but does not pull it from the water because now the soap lady is flat out sprinting across the lake in his direction. She leaves her feet with a minor jump and comes slapping back down in a skid on the water, twenty feet from him, fifteen feet, ten, hissing along the slick surface. My father holds the axe in his soap hand inches below the surface and fights to keep from lunging toward her in an all out ambush on the ghost-flesh.

And when she reaches my father, feet first, body arched in the shape of a Z, her skeletal arms held forward, my father heaves the hatchet up and brings it across the space between their bodies where the blade's keen edge catches the soap lady's outstretched left arm and slices through it with the surprising ease of trawling a spoon through milk. Her arm drops away into the water and the lake boils and the soap lady collapses on the beach, face down in the sand among oil cans, ashtrays, and Coke-can six-pack rings.

She doesn't cry or yell or screech or project her voice somewhere else, doesn't make a single sound but for the grating of her arms and legs on the sand. My father leaps onto her back and pins her hard body to the beach with his chest. He grabs her remaining arm, wrenches it behind her back. She is still warm, still dangerous. She squirms and bucks but cannot shove off the weight. He can steal off her other arm. He can hijack the legs at the kneebacks. Hell, he can go for the broomstick neck. But with all this, the hatchet, the arm, her stump, the greasy lake, his own son, me, the scalded trails down his bicep, the glint of a bottleneck farther down the shore where I'm hiding in the azaleas, with all of this in his head (and mine), he wants to leave her with nothing.

My father holds the knife-edge up close to her wounded shoulder and chips off a divot. The flaky chunk pops off. Nothing happens. Another piece; same result. And so he works away at her body with the precision of a sculptor, nicking off these white slivers and squares that go decorating the dirty sand. It does not take long. The faster he works, the sooner she disappears, until all that's left is a soap-spine and head. He gets on his knees, holds this last section up, and breaks it in his hands: even I can hear it snap. Then he looks down at his own new hand. He gives it another flex, admires it. And it is with this bright arm that he waves to me: it's okay, it's okay, I'm fine, you can come out now.

I run over, but stop halfway and stare him over, unsure. He bends down and waves again, this time with his real arm. I walk the rest of the way and touch his soap skin. It's no different than the Dial bar in our bathroom. To tell him I saw the whole thing, could tell exactly what he thought, even felt those hot hands, means nothing. I am worried about this new thing and how it will separate us.

Together we collect the white shavings in separate bags. I get to carry the hatchet home and that night we carve chess pieces out of the soap lady's bones and we take turns washing our hands after every single game.

Brad Vice

The Six Million Dollar Man VS. Jaws

His house is a wreck, socks and magazines all over the floors, dirty dishes stacked in the sink. On the ledge of the couch lies a splayed copy of *Entertainment Weekly,* reading *Roy Schneider Dead Age 75,* and Steven Austin, age 34—the manager of a beleaguered Radio Shack—is a man barely alive.

He has the flu—a bad one. He is so exhausted and so weak that he suspects this is no ordinary flu, but maybe some dreaded avian flu or even West Nile, or perhaps he will be one of the first cases of some brand new but statistically inevitable pandemic begun in China and set out to ravage the globe. Within the last year, he has missed almost two months of work for a series of self-diagnosed ailments including migraines, shortness of breath, joint paint, mysterious glandular swellings—in short, a constant and general lack of well being. Perhaps the stress of his job and his fraying marriage has reawakened the mono he contracted from kissing Gretchen Hornblower in the 8th grade, or perhaps it is CFS—Chronic Fatigue Syndrome, or fibromyalgia, or any number of other nebulous yet infinitely detailed conditions Steven has researched on the internet; or perhaps it is even the dreaded Multiple Myeloma that ravaged his father's immune system and killed the poor man dead only a few months after Steven married. That was ten years ago, and still there is no cure, nor so far as Steven knows even any improved treatment. "There are new medical technologies being invented everyday," the doctors had told his dad, looking up from their clipboards, projecting an air of reassuring rational optimism as they patted his shoulder. Yeah, right. They might as well have asked nicely, *Pretty please, with sugar on top, don't commit suicide,* after each chemo treatment. And now, MM has claimed a new victim—Chief "You're gonna need a bigger boat" Brody. Even the stars aren't safe.

Steven feels the rank cherry cough syrup hanging on his breath. Sketched out on decongestants, his hearts races, and yet he can't bring himself to get up off the couch to brush his teeth.

Steven wants to be cyborg, like his hero and namesake, Colonel Steve Austin, the Six Million Dollar Man. As a kid, Steven had watched reruns of the show with his dad, rapt as Lee Majors used his bionic limbs, his scientifically improved body, to do battle with Nazis, Communists, and aliens alike. Where are the scientists from the Pentagon, NASA, the OSI—the fabled Office of Scientific Intelligence? Where in the hell is Oscar Goldman when you need him?

Deep down Steven knows this flu is all in his mind, and yet this knowledge does nothing to make him better. Finally he drags himself off the couch and stumbles into the kitchen with the intent to load the dishwasher. He repeats his mantra, "We can rebuild him. Better, faster, stronger." "Better, faster, stronger." And yet he spends a full five minutes trying to focus the willpower to lift the plates crusted with tomato sauce and cheese out of the stainless steel sink. *Better, Faster, Stronger.* The words seem to circle the drain of the garbage disposal before they are sucked into the shadowy depths, where Steven can almost feel the maw of gears and teeth grinding them up.

Soon Dr. Wife will be home and discover the mess and they will fight. And Steven knows that in the battle between immuno-compromised Steven vs. Dr. Wife, he will lose. Who is he kidding? He would lose even on his best day. Dr. Wife is the AP biology teacher at Vaughn Academy Prep, paid extra for her Ph.D., and she herself will most certainly be exhausted from staving off the wheedling assaults of the privileged, A-hungry overachievers that swim the waters of her classroom. He should be more considerate. His hiatus from RadioShack is hurting them financially, but he just can't bear the thought of listening to all those questions about splicing cables and hooking up Xboxes to the surround sound. What happened to the future, he has often wondered? Stifled. Where are the silver space suits? The robots to do the house work? Where is, Steven wonders—*Where is my flying fucking car?* As a boy, it seemed he had almost been promised a flying car, from George Jetson's daily commute to Buck Rogers's 25th century skyways. Even dreary, hard boiled Harrison Ford got to ride in a flying car in the dystopian San Francisco of *Blade Runner*. When things are pressed to the wall at the Shack, Steven ponders the empty promises made by the future. All around him only cables and adapters, tools made to repair frayed or antiquated connections.

As an employee in the service industry, he has asked, "How may I help you?" so many times he now sometimes murmurs it in his sleep as he tosses and turns in troubled dreams. His Major Tom dreams, he calls them. Always through the docking bay windows of his space ship, a faceless astronaut floats away from Steven, floating in cold space, floating farther and farther away from the safety of the ship. Alone at the control panel, Steven finds every button and light is frozen. Anchored only by the umbilicus of the oxygen tube connected to his suit, the lost astronaut is pulled farther and farther into space, caught in some invisible undertow dragging him into the depths outside the window of Steven's console where no one can hear his cries for help. The blank stare of the visor recedes farther and farther to the frozen vacuum until the astronaut is as tiny as a baby, a doll, a dot, and then nothing. "How can I help you?" screams Steven, over and over again, only to wake to find Dr. Wife snoring soundly.

Standing over the sink of dirty dishes, Steven knows he has been presented with a false choice, to be helpful or not to be helpful. It doesn't matter. Regardless of what he does, Steven and Dr. Wife will inevitably be drawn into further conflict. The last fight had begun as a dispute about dirty dishes, about the proper way to load the dishwasher—Steven had front-loaded a casserole dish in the top rack. This deviation ended in an argument so absurd as to stretch the bounds of plausibility. Who would win in a fight? The Six Million Dollar Man or the shark from *Jaws*?

"In a boat or in the water?" asked Dr. Wife. She was a blunt woman with beautifully white skin and a perfectly symmetrical face. She would have been a beautiful woman if she had not been born a scientist. She preferred clubbed shoes and an almost comically utilitarian hair style reminiscent of the *Peanuts* character Marcie. Dr. Wife often used blunt logic to get her way. From the outset of their last melee, Steven could see she was already calculating two rhetorical strategies simultaneously.

"In a boat or on the water?"

"Either way," shrugged Steven in an attempt at evasion. He was clutching his fifth grade lunchbox, the one with Col. Steve Austin in a puffy white space suit on the thermos. He had placed it on the tabletop of the wooden high chair that sat in the corner beside the fridge. The chair was an heirloom, built by his grandfather, and both Steven and his father had sat in it. Up until the last few weeks he had hoped to get some further use out of it. Dr. Wife had suffered another miscarriage; she endured the D and E with stoic, almost stoned-heart bravery. "This is nature's way of keeping us from having a retard," said Dr. Wife with a bit of a comic sneer after the scrape and vacuum. And it was with this sneer that she later made her case for the shark.

"You think the Six Million Dollar Man can take a forty-foot rogue great white, in open water?"

Steven inspected all four sides of his lunch box as if consulting some sort of reference material. "Colonel Steve Austin is one of the greatest Americans to ever to become a US Air Force Test Pilot. The man walked on the moon. After the bionic implants, he could run sixty miles per hour, jump tall buildings in a single bound, punch through cinder blocks and bend steel with his right arm, which has the power of a bulldozer. His left eye allows him a 20 to one zoom ratio vision, night vision, infrared. He *is* a classified top secret weapon of the OSI. How can you even say The Six Million Dollar Man would lose at anything? You've never even seen the show."

"What are bionics anyway?"

"Biological Electronics."

"Uh-uh. And OSI?"

"The Office of Scientific Intelligence."

"Oooooooh, sounds important," said Dr. Wife. "Sounds like something made up by a bunch of goobers who hang out at RadioShack. Geeks without the imagination to join Star Fleet Academy. Horny dorks dreaming of a future where they will get laid."

Steven squinted. He was angry now. "Colonel Steve Austin took on everything from aliens to Big Foot. You don't think he can handle a shark?"

"Infrared vision? Sharks can sense the base electrical impulses generated by any living being. Their sense of smell can detect blood in the water miles away. One part per million, registers in their nervous system and attracts them. They never sleep. They don't dream of a future where they are strong and powerful. All they do is swim and eat and make little sharks. Six million dollars? What the hell is six million dollars compared to complete evolutionary fucking perfection?"

"Look, first of all Steve Austin was made in like nineteen seventy-three. So if you adjust for inflation…." Steven trotted into the living room, and opened his laptop, signed on to the wireless, and Googled a financial calculator. With help of hundreds of satellites and millions of high frequency radio waves operating in concordance, he performed a complicated mathematical equation, and adjusted for inflation. He returned to the kitchen five minutes later, triumphant, "He would be, like, the 27,931,682 dollar and 42 cent Man, today." Steven emphasized the word *man* as if he were adding the final mark of punctuation to some seminal document, one that would later foment a technical as well a cultural revolution.

"Do you know how long the great white has been swimming around its current conformature? Three hundred million years. They have found teeth from prehistoric sharks as big as your hand. The extinct *Megalodon Carcharodon* probably isn't even extinct. It was probably just a really big ass great white unimpeded by current limiting factors to growth. Sharks don't get their feelings hurt. They don't pout. They don't suffer depression, or anxiety attacks, or hypochondria, *Steven*. They don't even get cancer."

My God, was she making fun of his father? Had she realized how enumerating these simple facts would make him feel? They don't get cancer. And now Chief Brody dead with MM. Gonna need a bigger boat. Absolutely, Goddamn, Right. New technologies are being invented every day, say the oncologists. Right.

Steven took a deep breath and lowered his eyes pondering all the things he'd lost in the last few years, his dad, his baby, his confidence, his self respect. Now standing over the dirty dishes soaking in the sink, Steven begins to ponder the aquatic battle between his hero and the shark. The Six Million Dollar Man vs. Jaws. Cyborg vs. Monster of the Deep. Maimed Captain vs. Leviathan. One punch to the nose with his bionic arm and the shark would lose all of his teeth . . . but shark teeth always grow back, don't they? Maybe the monster would simply swallow the mechanical arm and its owner's torso whole before the powerful bulldozer fist made contact. One kick to the gills and the shark would roll over and suffocate in the water like giant gurgling infant with its throat crushed. Or would the shark evade all contact with his prey until the man tired, tired less quickly than his other prey perhaps, yes, but in an infinite ocean, wouldn't even the bionic man tire, sink, drown, or at the very least swim, paddle, and splash with his mechanical arms and legs until his human heart simply gave out.

ORGO vs the Flatlanders

BY PINCKNEY BENEDICT

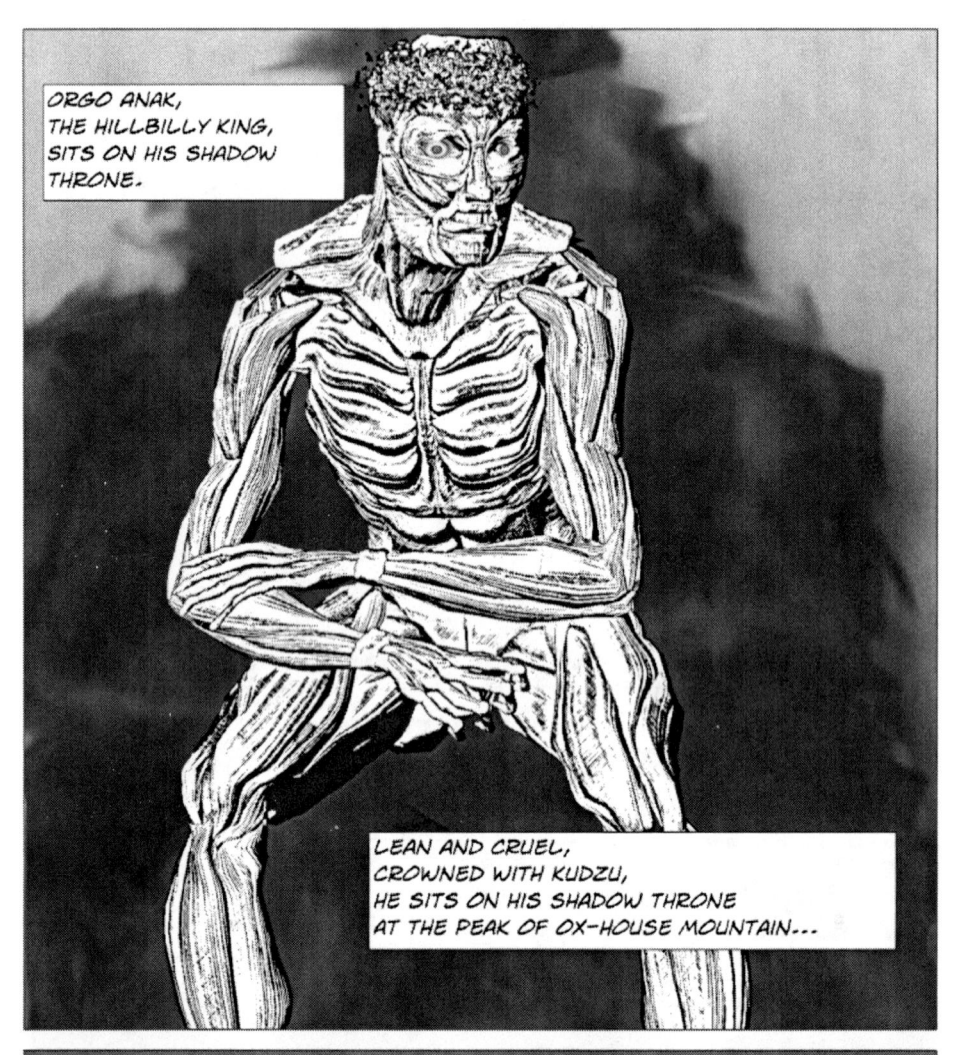

ORGO ANAK,
THE HILLBILLY KING,
SITS ON HIS SHADOW
THRONE.

LEAN AND CRUEL,
CROWNED WITH KUDZU,
HE SITS ON HIS SHADOW THRONE
AT THE PEAK OF OX-HOUSE MOUNTAIN...

...AND HE WAITS.

Orgo vs. The Flatlanders 17

THE MEN OF THE MOUNTAINS HATE THE MEN OF THE FLATLANDS WITH A KILLING HATRED.

THIS IS THE HATRED THAT TURNS THE WORLD.

THIS IS THE HATRED THAT BRINGS THE NIGHT.

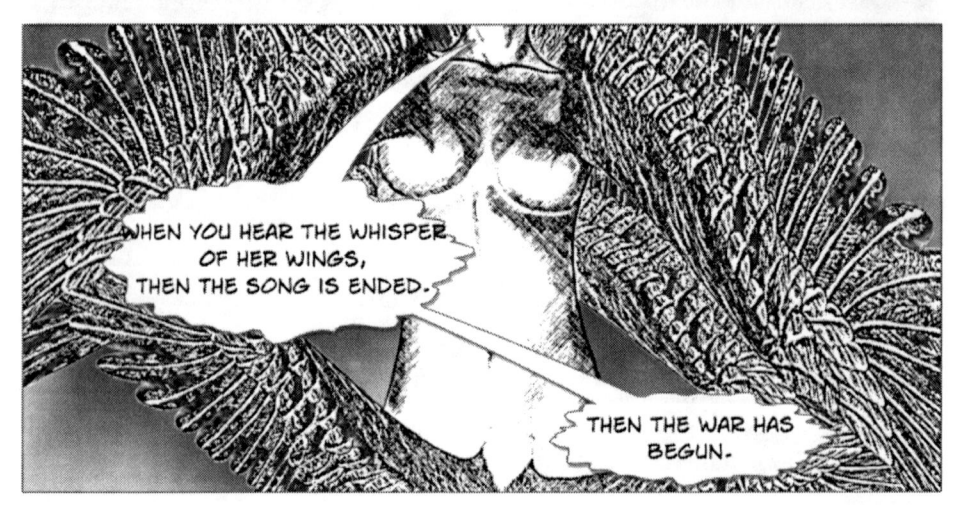

WHO SINGS THE SONG OF ORGILUS GRACILIS, LAST OF THE ANAKIM? OF ORGO ANAK, THE HILLBILLY KING?

WHO SINGS THE SONG OF HIS HATRED?

MOTHER DUST SINGS THE SONG.

WHEN YOU HEAR THE WHISPER OF HER WINGS, THEN THE SONG IS ENDED.

THEN THE WAR HAS BEGUN.

Orgo vs. The Flatlanders 19

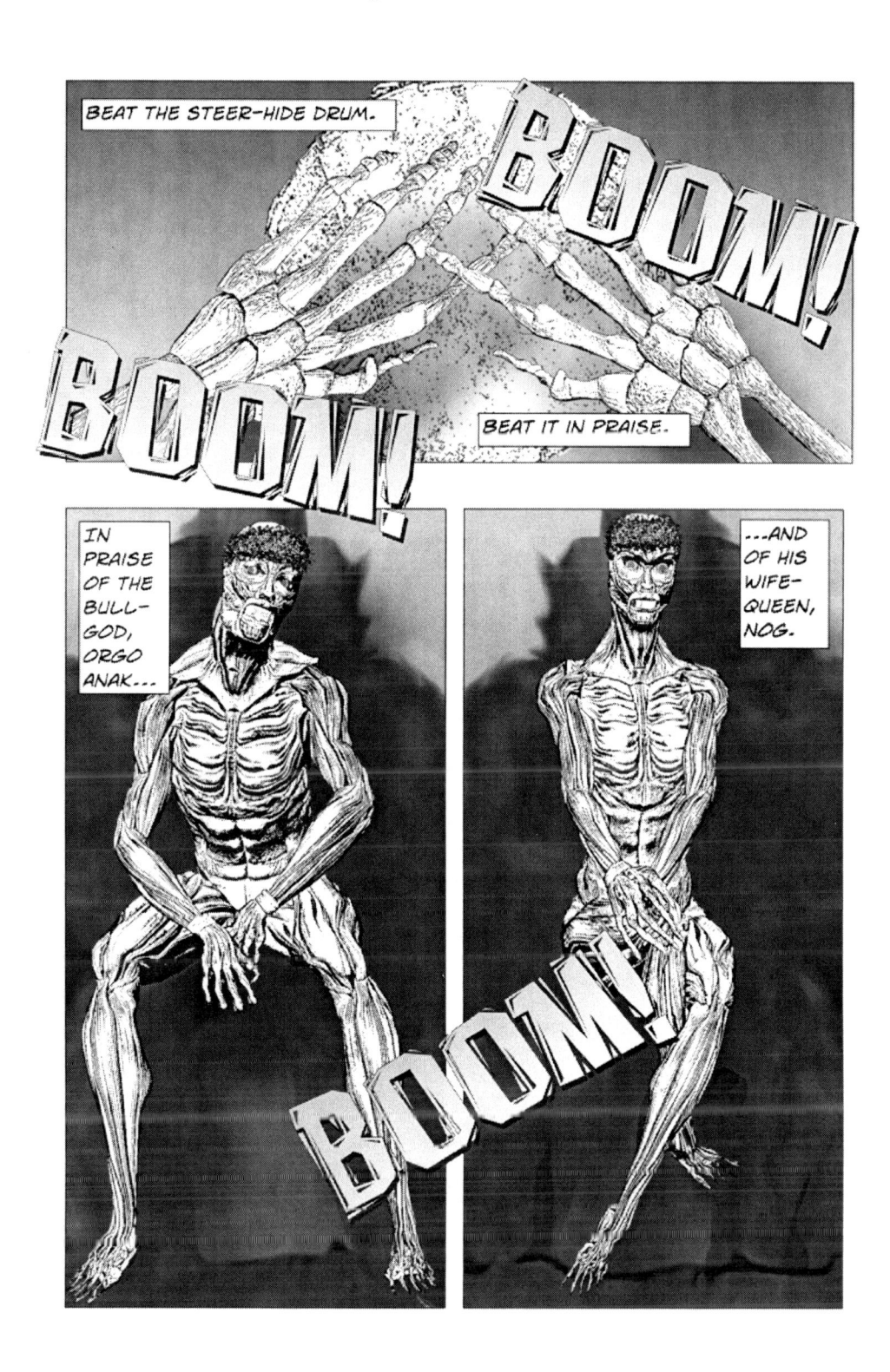

BEAT THE STEER-HIDE DRUM.

BOOM!

BOOM!

BEAT IT IN PRAISE.

IN PRAISE OF THE BULL-GOD, ORGO ANAK...

...AND OF HIS WIFE-QUEEN, NOG.

BOOM!

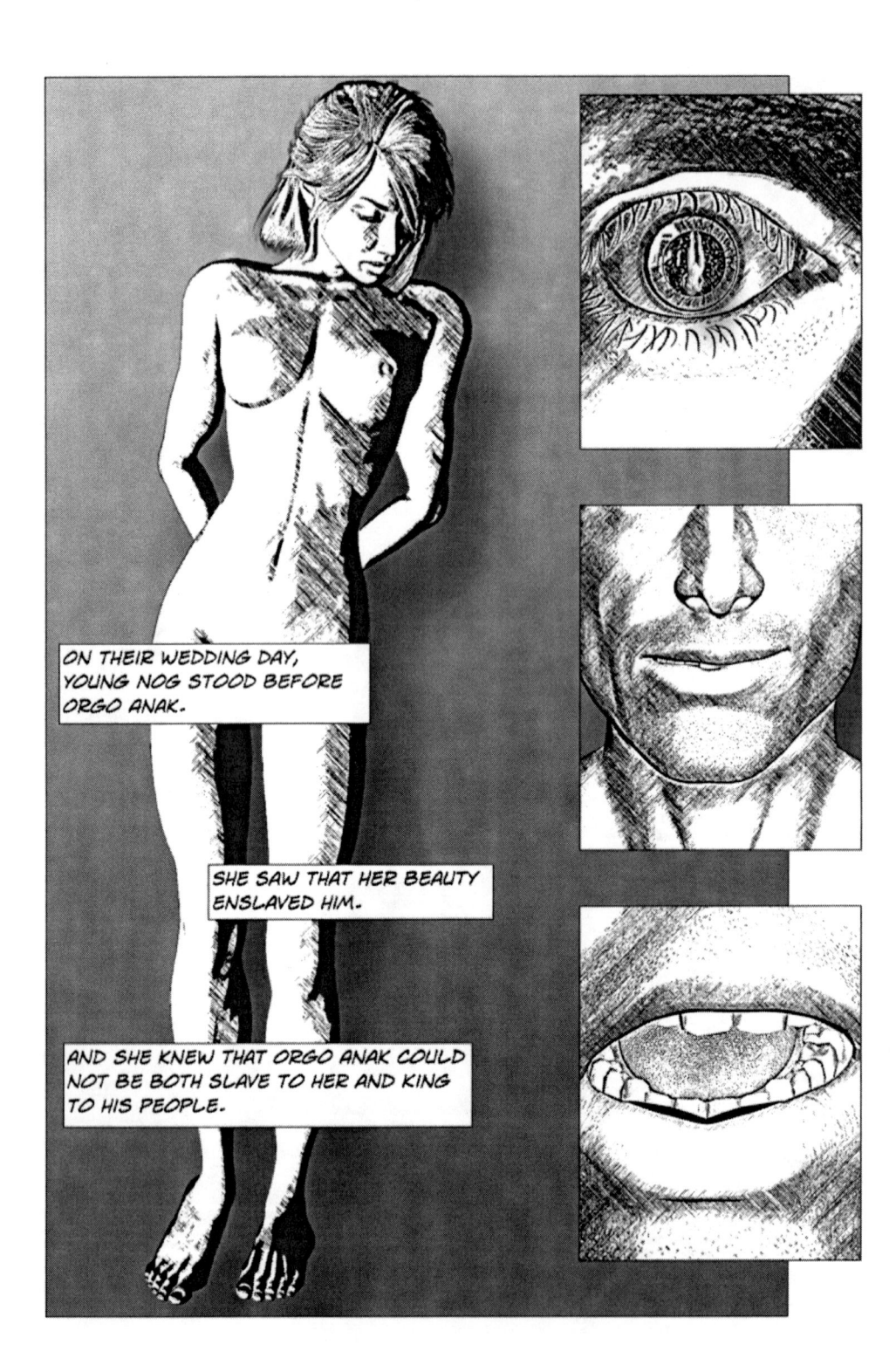

ON THEIR WEDDING DAY, YOUNG NOG STOOD BEFORE ORGO ANAK.

SHE SAW THAT HER BEAUTY ENSLAVED HIM.

AND SHE KNEW THAT ORGO ANAK COULD NOT BE BOTH SLAVE TO HER AND KING TO HIS PEOPLE.

Orgo vs. The Flatlanders 21

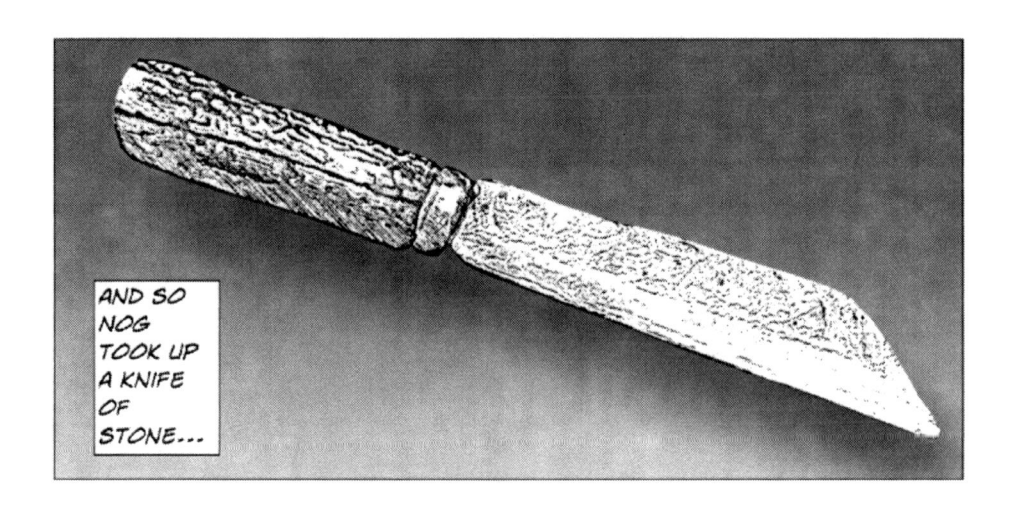

AND SO NOG TOOK UP A KNIFE OF STONE...

...AND PEELED HER OWN SKIN AWAY.

SEEING WHAT NOG HAD DONE, ORGO THEN TOOK A KNIFE OF COLD IRON...
...AND SKINNED HIMSELF...
...THAT THEY MIGHT RULE TOGETHER.

Orgo vs. The Flatlanders 23

THEY LEFT BEHIND THEM THEIR HOME ON THE WINDSWEPT PLATEAU.

THEY LEFT BEHIND THEM...

...EVERYTHING.

Orgo vs. The Flatlanders 25

THEY SEARCHED OUT THE HIGH DESOLATE FASTNESS —

THE CLEFT IN THE ROCK —

THE SHADOW THRONE —

THE PLACE OF THE ALEPH —

- WHICH IS THE BULL THAT GAZES OUT FROM THE UNSEARCHABLE DEPTHS OF TIME.

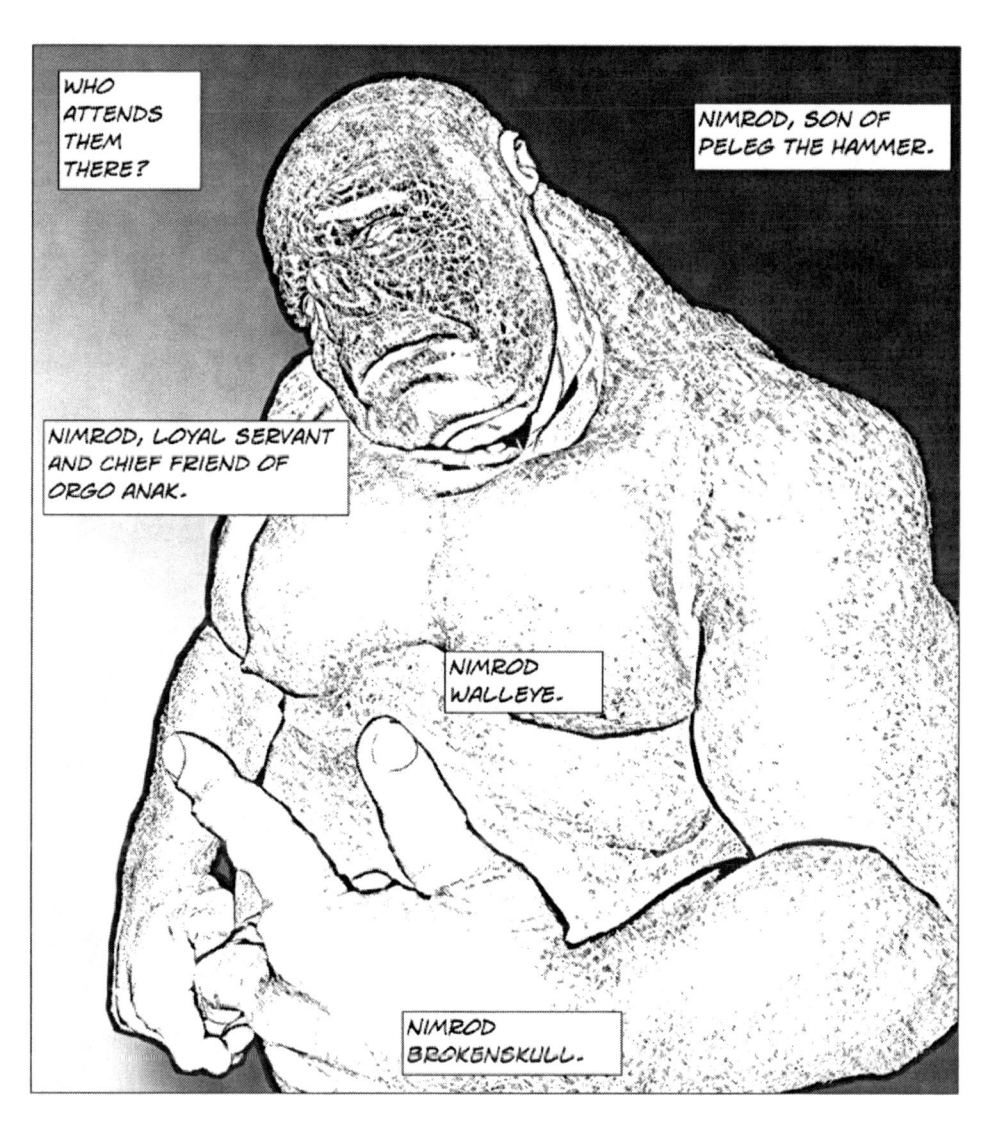

Orgo vs. The Flatlanders 27

> WHO ATTENDS THEM THERE?

> NIMROD, SON OF PELEG THE HAMMER.

> NIMROD, LOYAL SERVANT AND CHIEF FRIEND OF ORGO ANAK.

> NIMROD WALLEYE.

> NIMROD BROKENSKULL.

> HE ALONE MAY LOOK UPON THEM...

> ...BECAUSE HIS EYES ARE DIM.

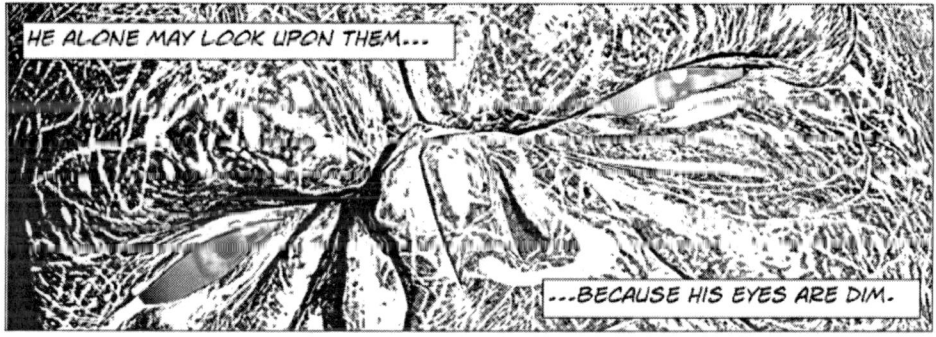

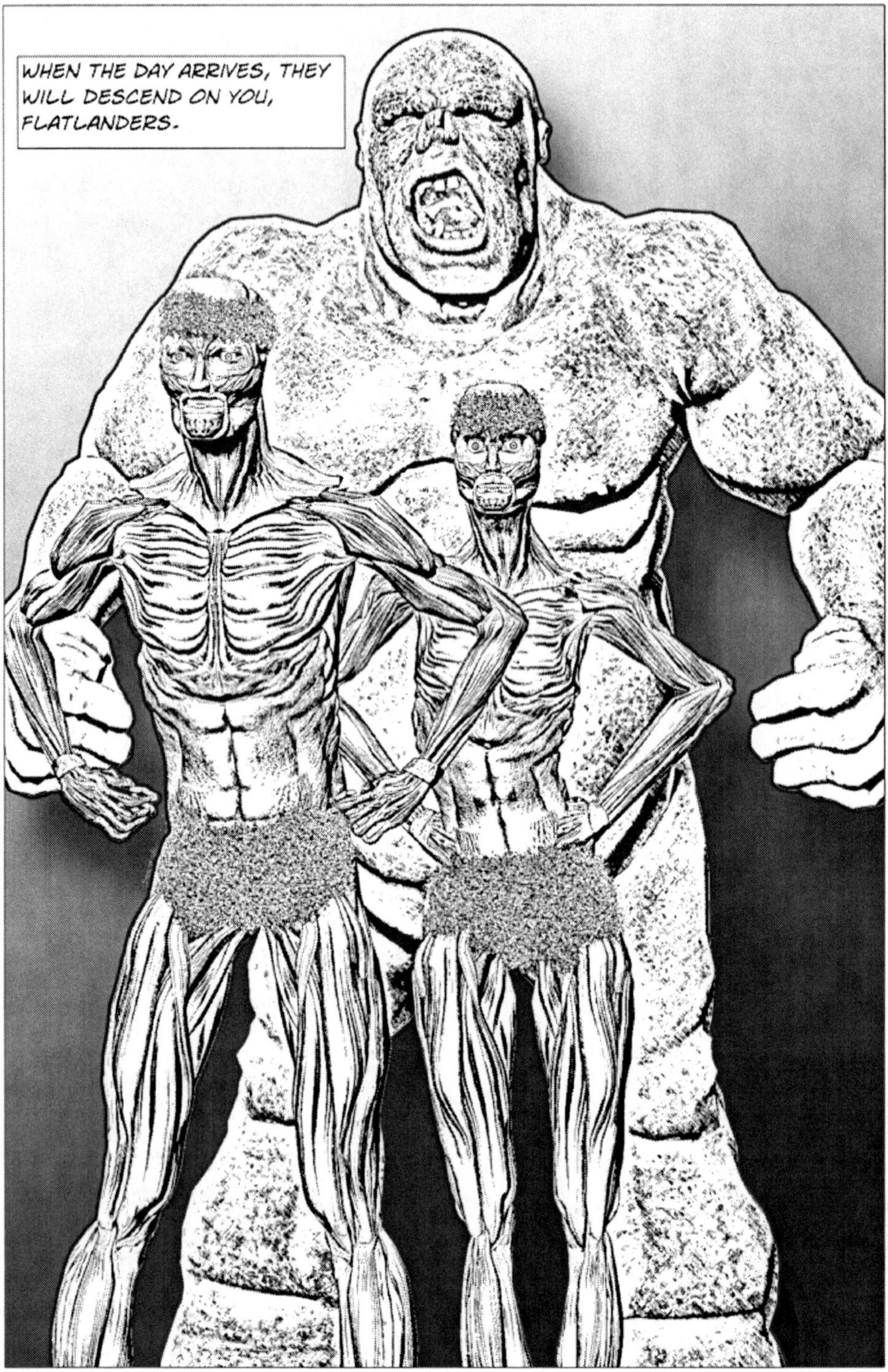
WHEN THE DAY ARRIVES, THEY WILL DESCEND ON YOU, FLATLANDERS.

Orgo vs. The Flatlanders

WHEN WILL THAT MARVELOUS DAY ARRIVE?

WHEN THE BULL-GOD ORGO ANAK HAS BRED UPON HIS WIFE QUEEN NOG AN ARMY OF THEIR SONS.

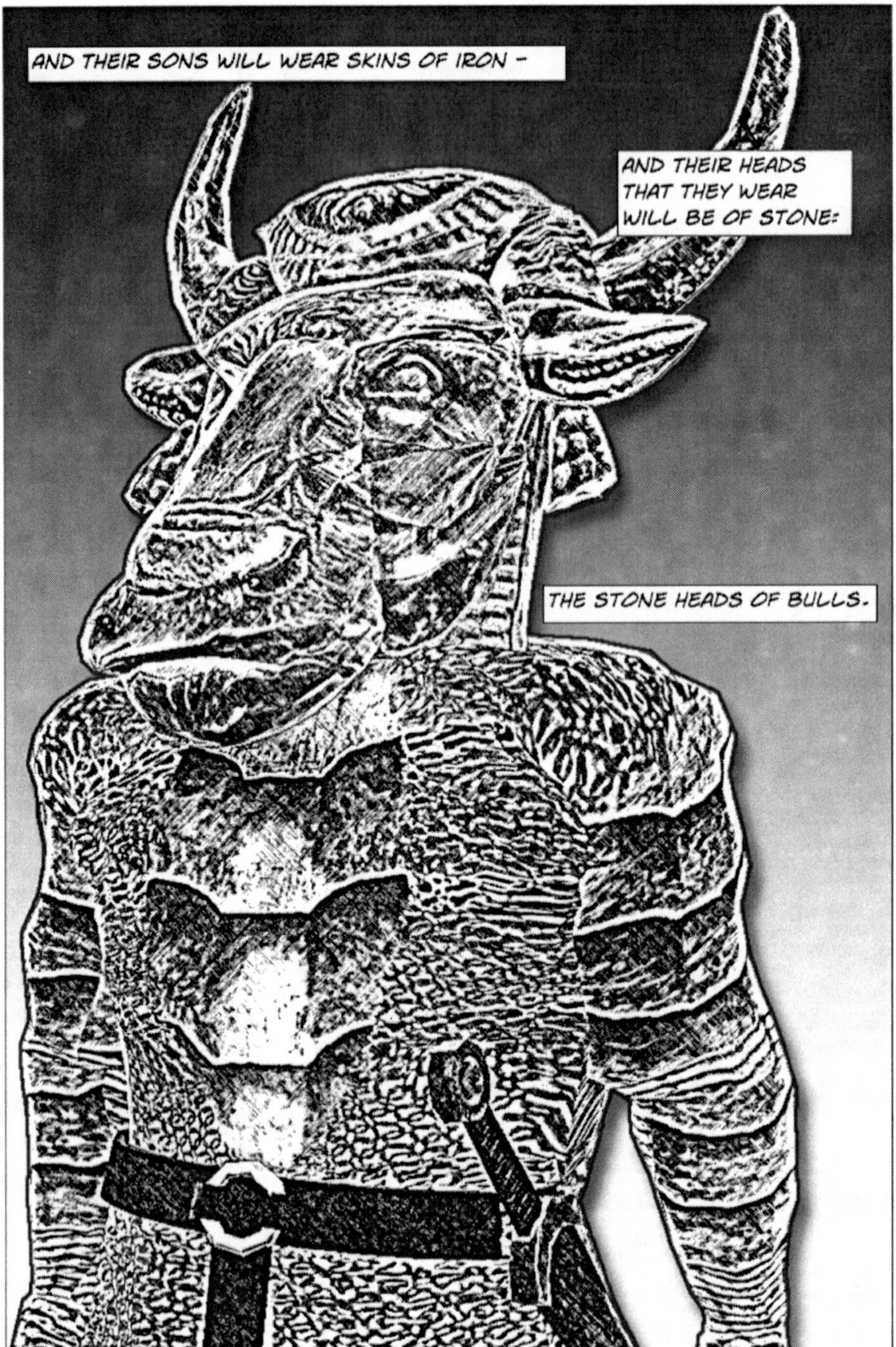
AND THEIR SONS WILL WEAR SKINS OF IRON -
AND THEIR HEADS THAT THEY WEAR WILL BE OF STONE:
THE STONE HEADS OF BULLS.

Orgo vs. The Flatlanders 31

AND WILL THE SONS OF ORGO GET DOWN?

YES.

THEY WILL GET DOWN.

YOU FEEL SAFE, DON'T YOU?
O PEOPLE OF THE FLATLANDS
SHELTERING IN YOUR TOWERS OF GLASS.

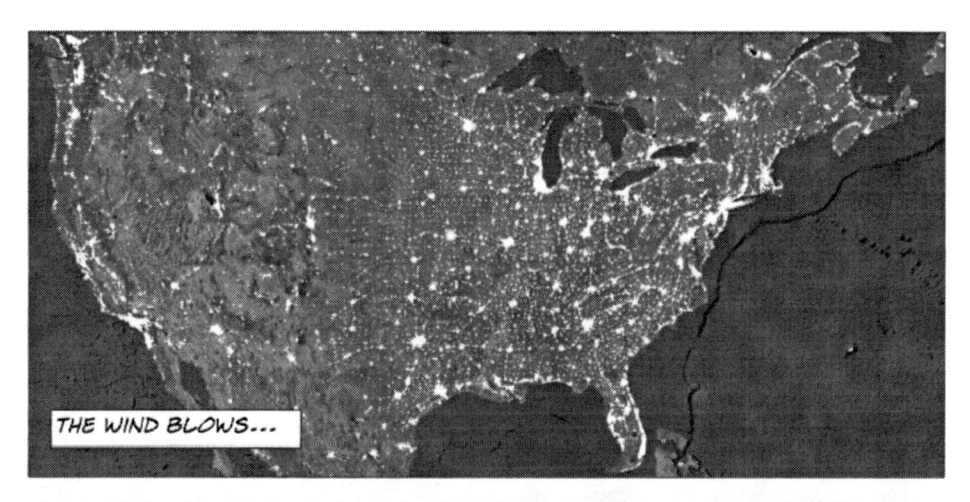

Orgo vs. The Flatlanders 33

THE WIND BLOWS...

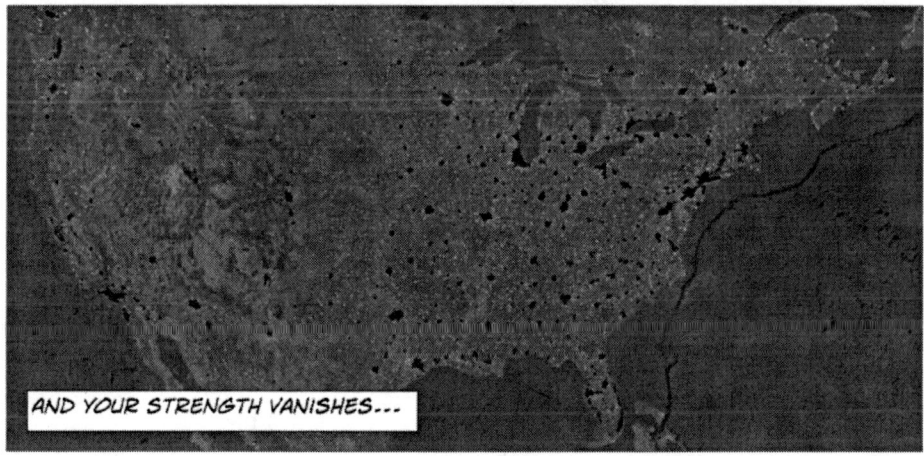

AND YOUR STRENGTH VANISHES...

UTTERLY.

ORGO ANAK HAS SEEN YOU.

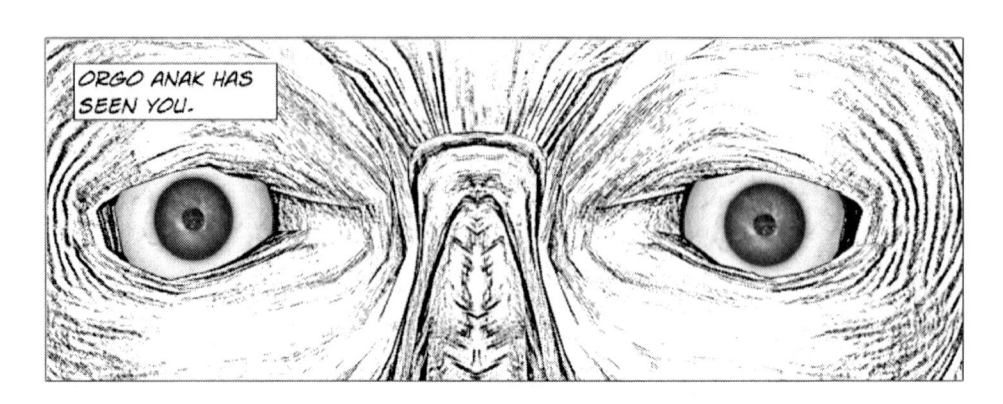

HE HAS SEEN YOUR TANGLED, INTOLERABLE CITIES.

Orgo vs. The Flatlanders 35

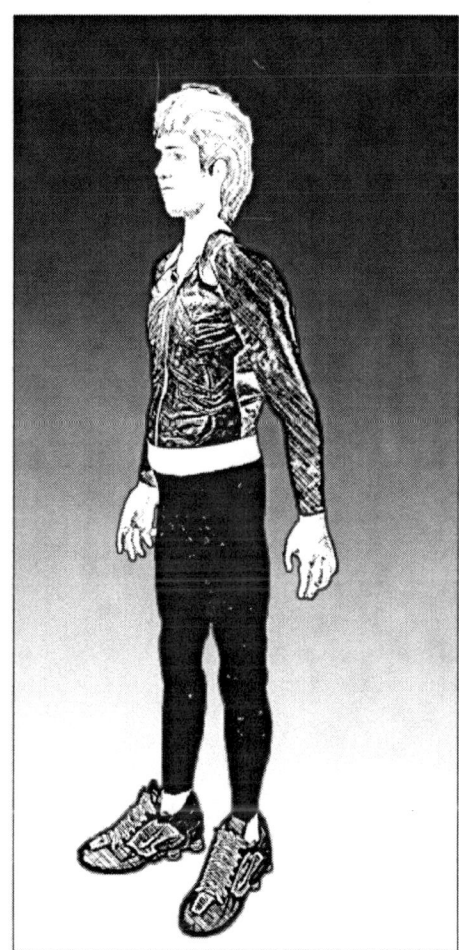

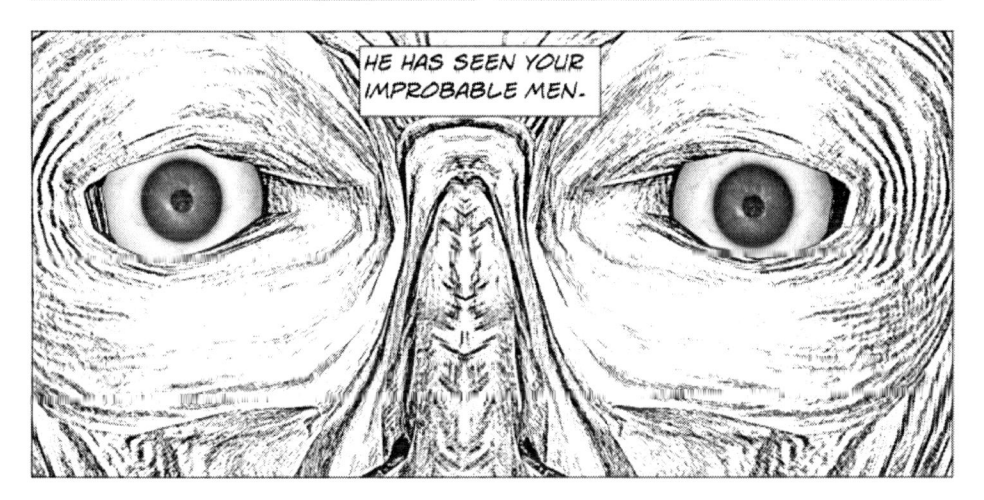

HE HAS SEEN YOUR IMPROBABLE MEN.

HE HAS SEEN YOUR IMPOSSIBLE WOMEN.
WHICH OF THEM –
– WILL TAKE HER SKIN OFF FOR YOU?

Orgo vs. The Flatlanders

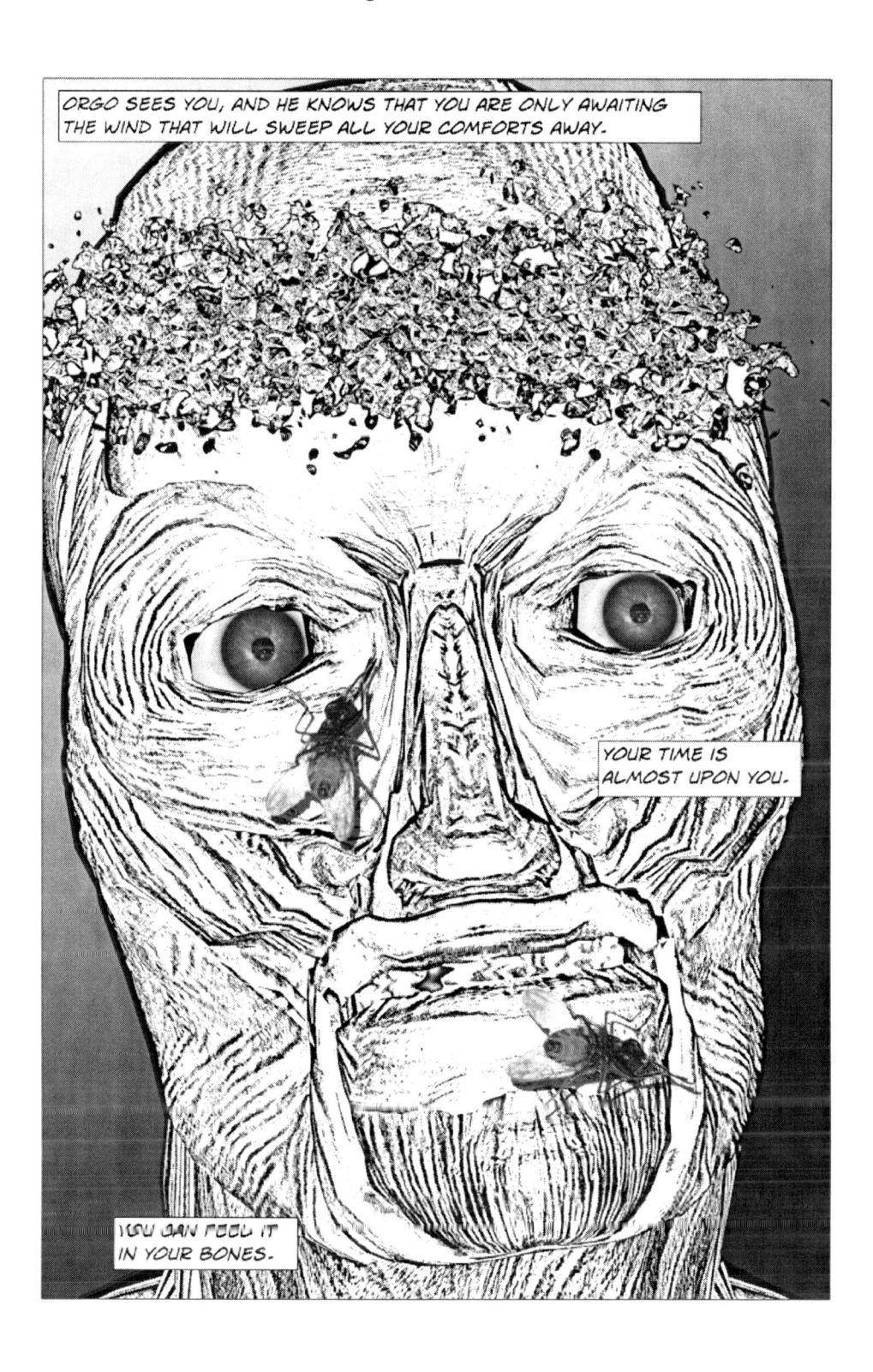

THE GEARS AND WHEELS THAT DRIVE THE FLATLANDS WILL GRIND TO A SLOW AND SHUDDERING HALT.

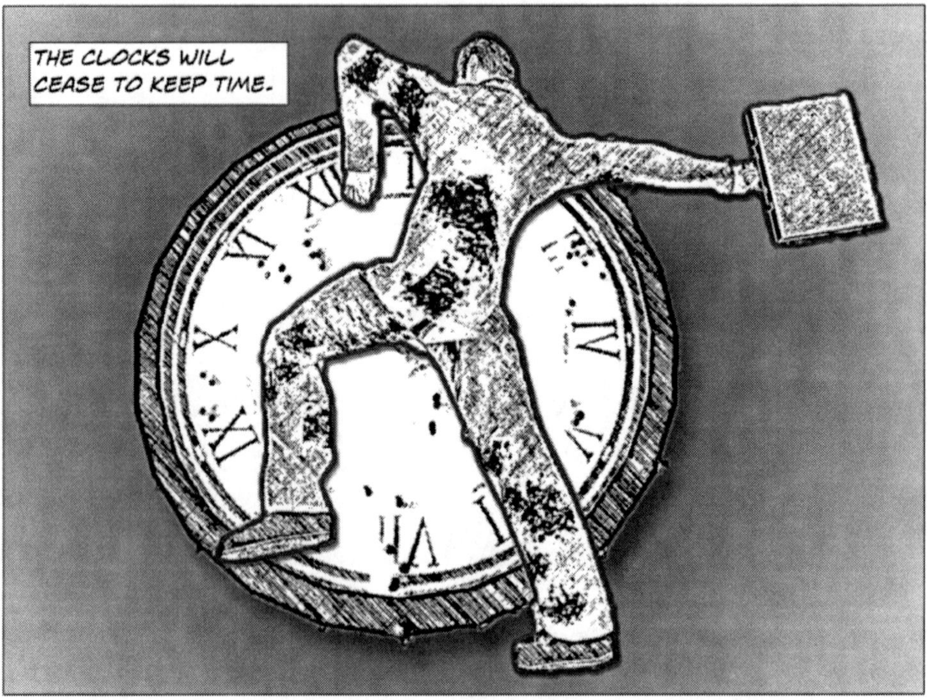
THE CLOCKS WILL CEASE TO KEEP TIME.

Orgo vs. The Flatlanders 39

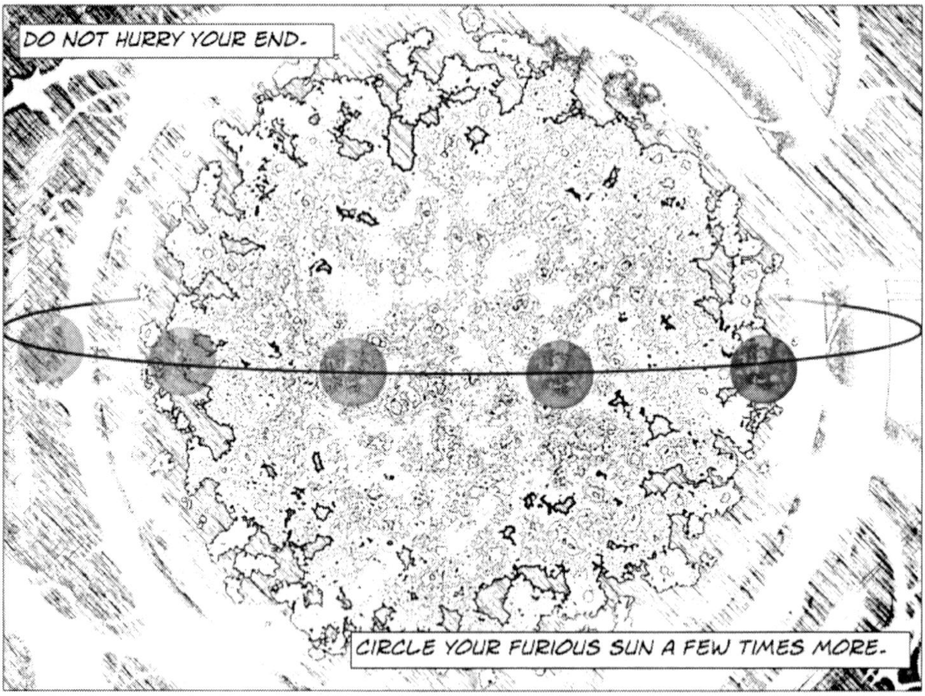
DO NOT HURRY YOUR END.
CIRCLE YOUR FURIOUS SUN A FEW TIMES MORE.

TIME PASSES WITH AGONIZING SLOWNESS ON THE CLOUDED SUMMIT OF OX-HOUSE MOUNTAIN.
THERE IS NO NEED TO RUSH.

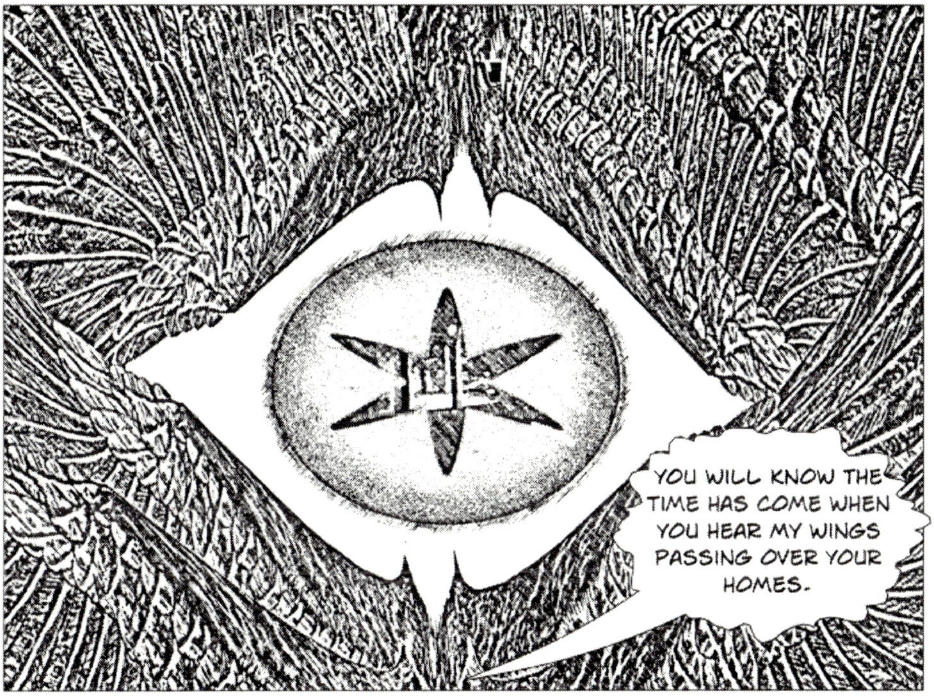
YOU WILL KNOW THE TIME HAS COME WHEN YOU HEAR MY WINGS PASSING OVER YOUR HOMES.

THEN, AT LAST, THE ARMY OF THE ALEPH WILL DESCEND UPON YOU.

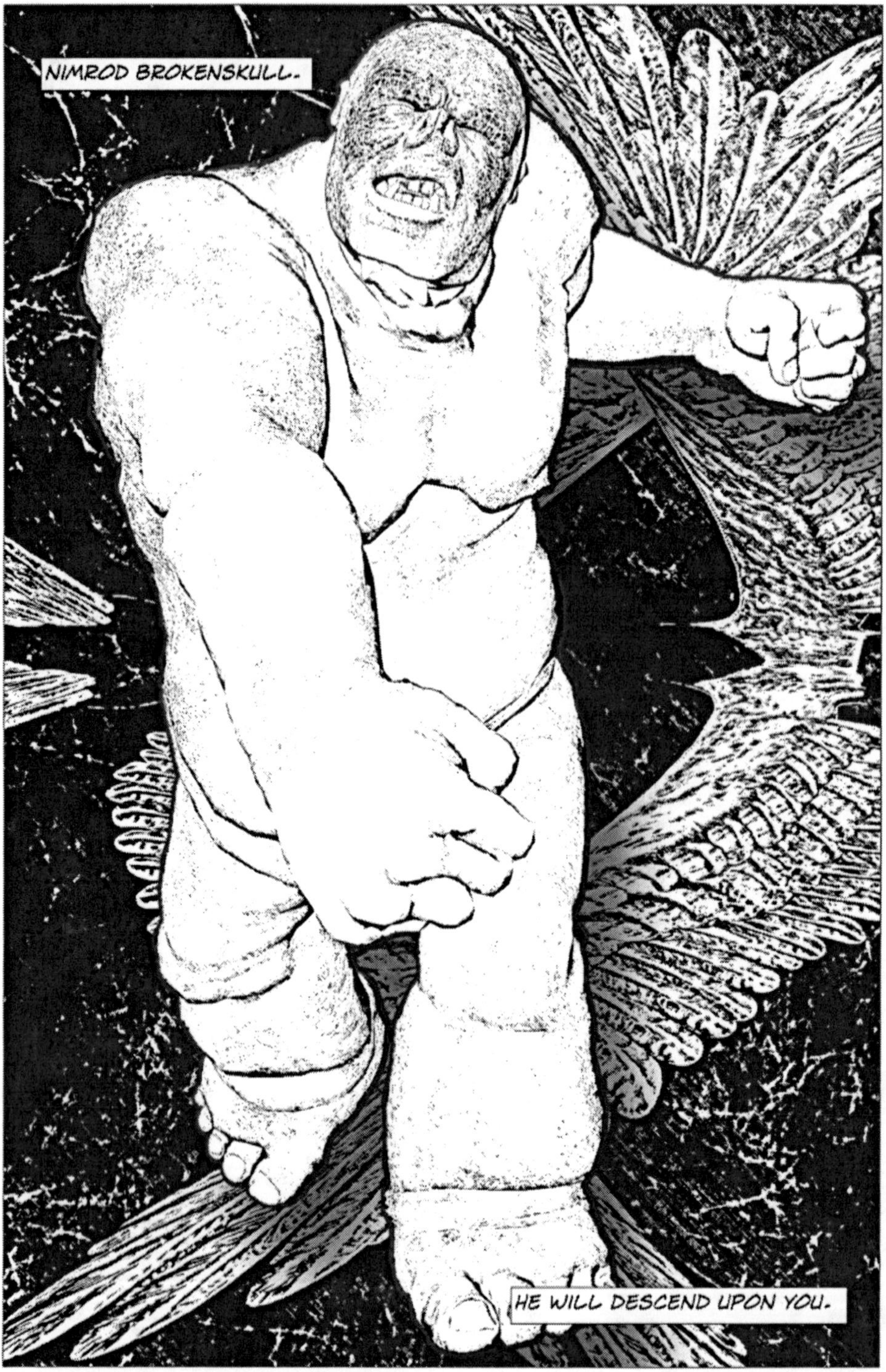
NIMROD BROKENSKULL.
HE WILL DESCEND UPON YOU.

Orgo vs. The Flatlanders 43

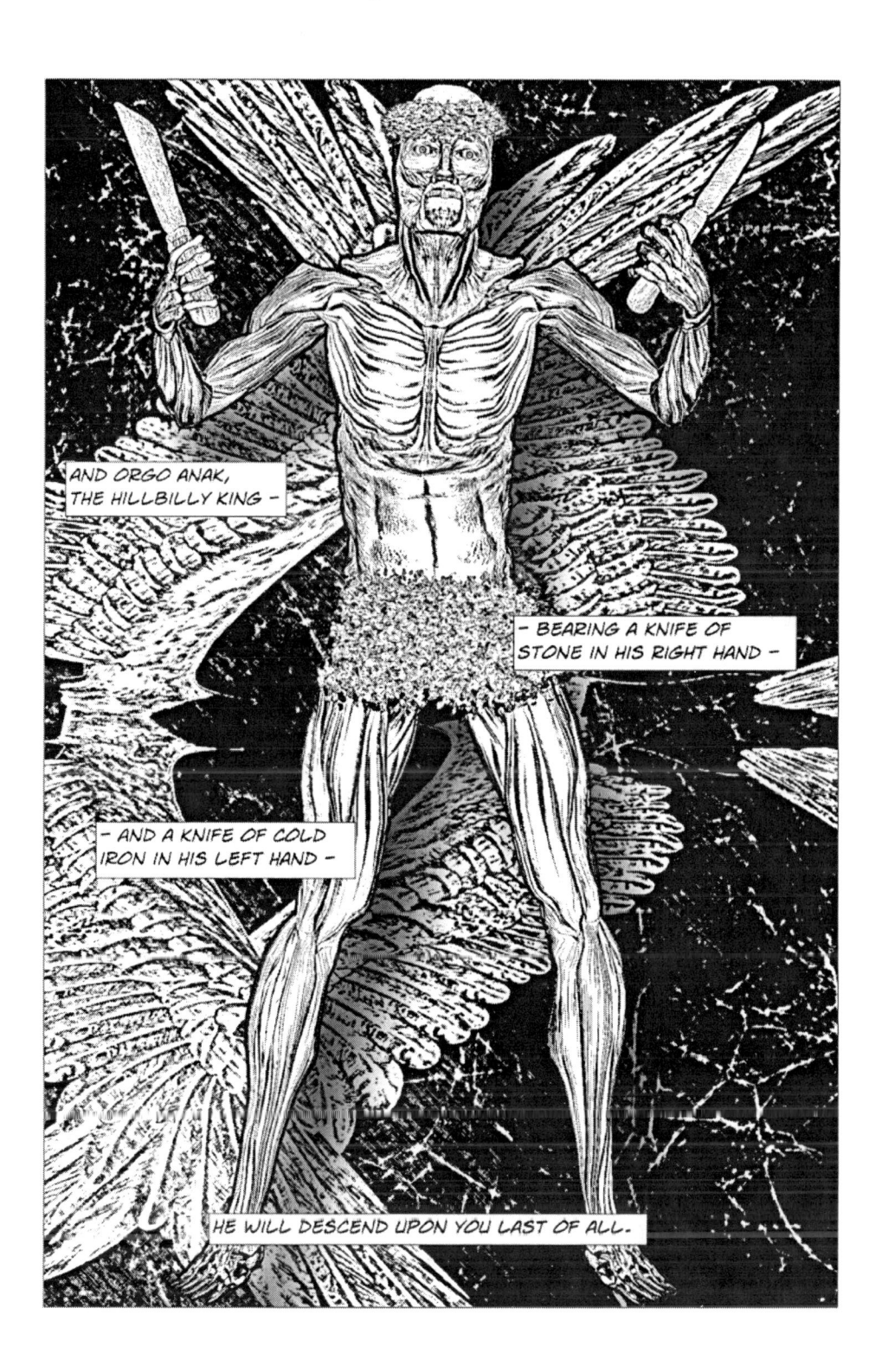

AND ORGO ANAK, THE HILLBILLY KING —

— BEARING A KNIFE OF STONE IN HIS RIGHT HAND —

— AND A KNIFE OF COLD IRON IN HIS LEFT HAND —

HE WILL DESCEND UPON YOU LAST OF ALL.

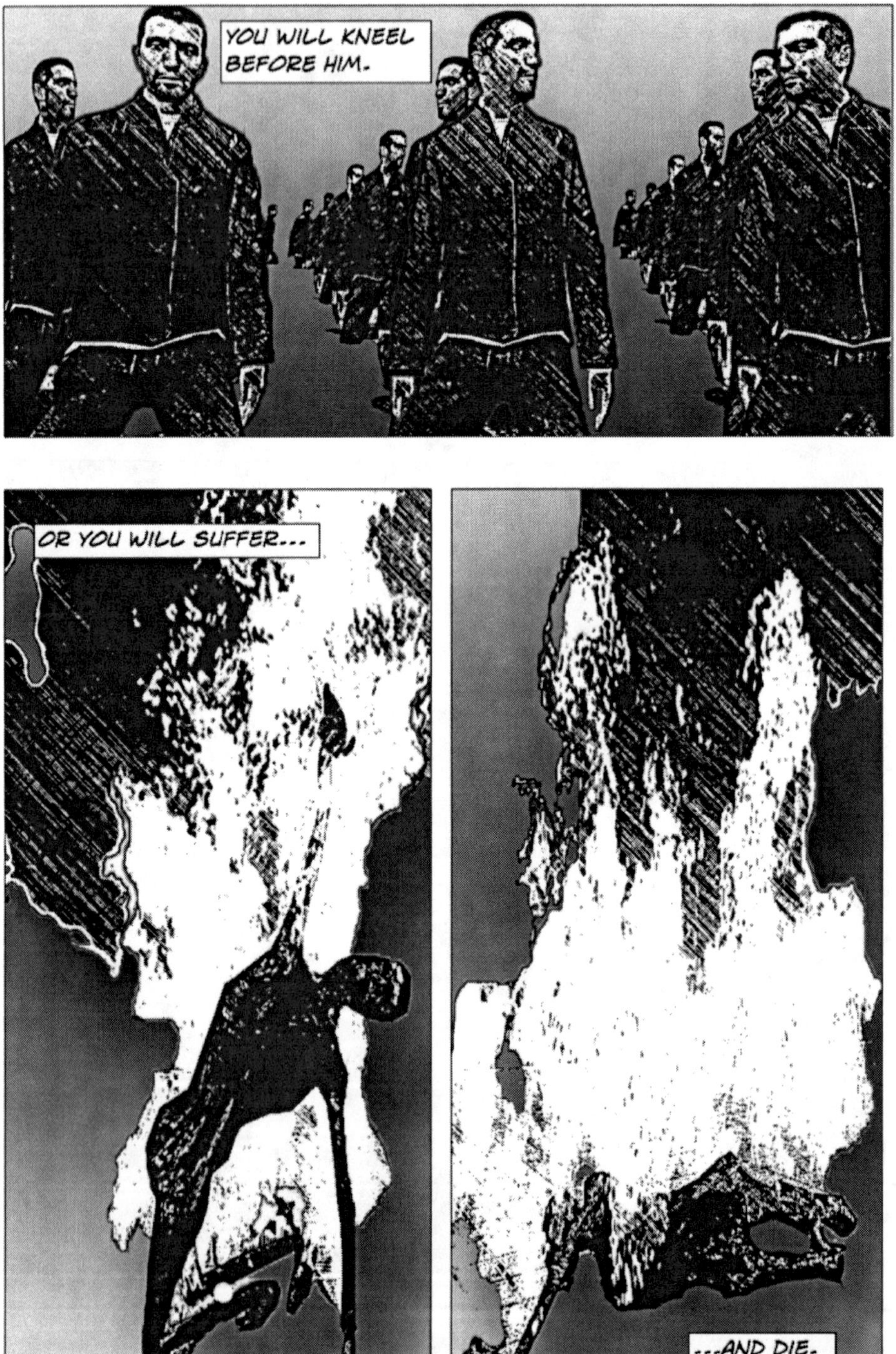
YOU WILL KNEEL
BEFORE HIM.
OR YOU WILL SUFFER...
...AND DIE.

Orgo vs. The Flatlanders 45

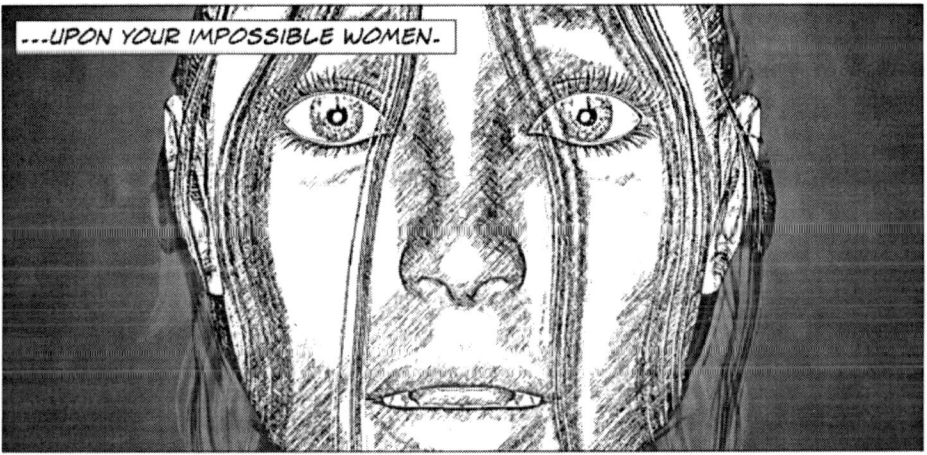

THE BULLHEADED SONS OF ORGO ANAK...

...WILL GET THEIR OWN STRONG SONS...

...UPON YOUR IMPOSSIBLE WOMEN.

NIMROD WILL TAKE HIMSELF
A NUMBER OF BRIDES.

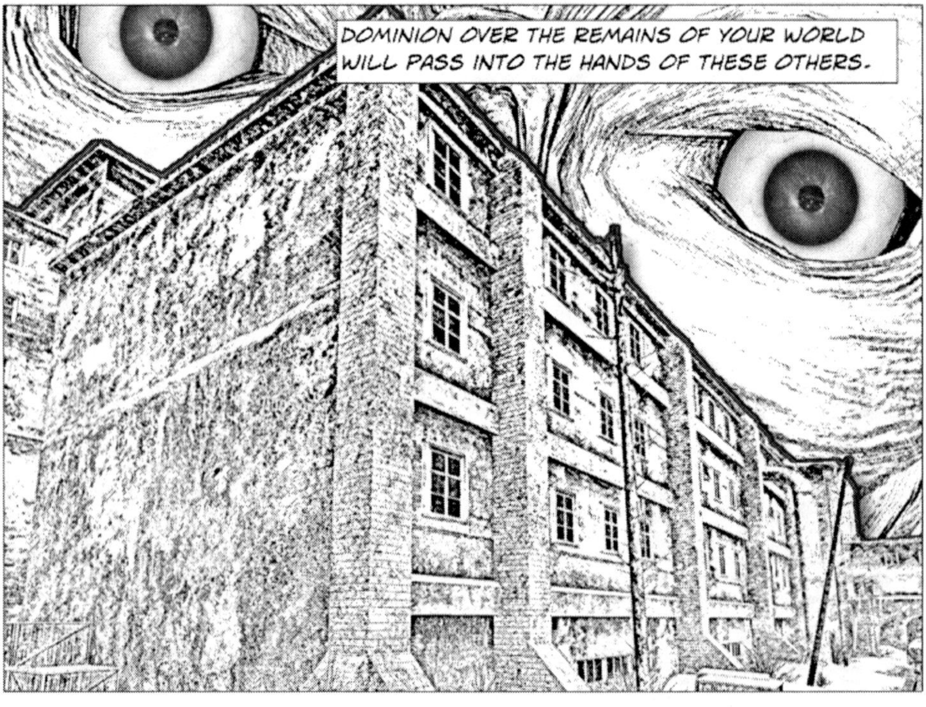
DOMINION OVER THE REMAINS OF YOUR WORLD
WILL PASS INTO THE HANDS OF THESE OTHERS.

Orgo vs. The Flatlanders

ONLY THEN WILL ORGO ANAK, THE HILLBILLY KING, DOFF HIS LEAFY CROWN.

ONLY THEN WILL HE GENTLY EMBRACE HIS WIFE-QUEEN, NOG —

AND HIS PASSION WILL CONSUME THEM BOTH.

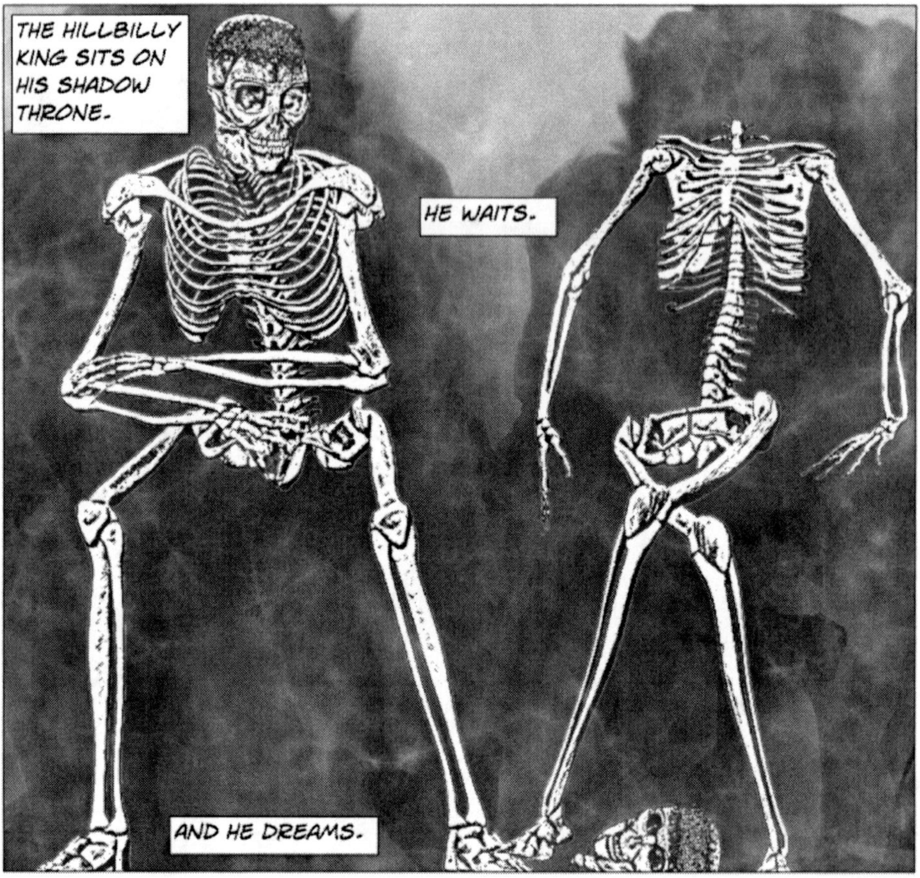
THE HILLBILLY KING SITS ON HIS SHADOW THRONE.
HE WAITS.
AND HE DREAMS.

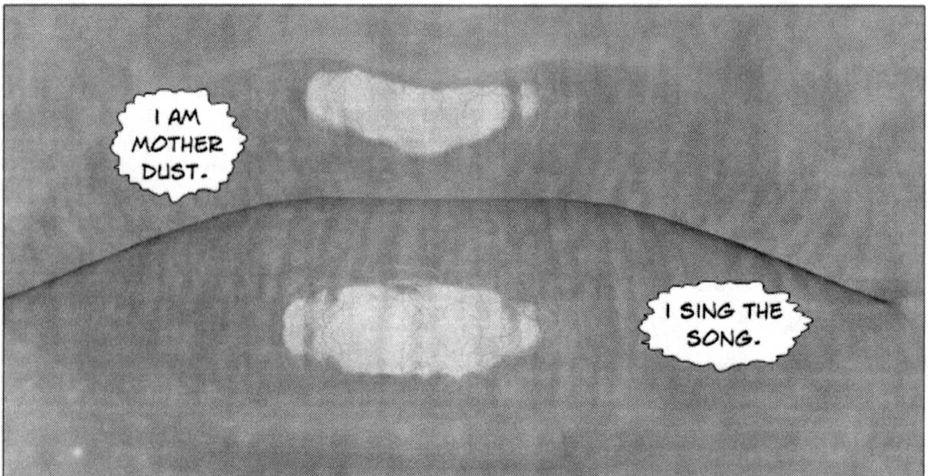
I AM MOTHER DUST.
I SING THE SONG.

John McNally

THE DEVIL'S ADVOCATE: MOE HOWARD VS. MOTHER TERESA

Many chance meetings between famous figures of the 19th and 20th centuries have been well-documented, but one such meeting would have disappeared from history altogether if not for the perseverance of a single scholar whose life's work was to connect the dots of one of the more bizarre feuds of the last century.

The following papers were found in the files of postdoctoral fellow James Tuttle, who died in 1998 under suspicious circumstances before he could finish his exhaustive study of the Vatican's influence over American pop culture of the 20th century. As Mr. Tuttle's literary executor, I offer no interpretations, though some might argue that my selection of these documents out of the over-ten-thousand pages in Dr. Tuttle's collection is a form, in and of itself, of interpretation. I refute this. I am neither a critic nor a scholar. I would prefer that these documents, which span forty-three years, speak for themselves.

DOCUMENT #1

```
                    Police Department
                    City of New York

                        Date    105          19   29

    Complainant       Agnes Bojaxhiu
    Address    No Permanent Address - Visiting from Ireland
    Offense       Assault
```

```
Reported By_____Same as Above_____
Address_____
Date and Time Offense Committed  10-5-29 6:30 p.m.
Place of Occurrence    42nd and Broadway_____
Person or Property Attacked  Sam Horwitz(aka Shemp Howard
How Attacked  Beaten with fists, verbally assaulted
Person Wanted   Moses Horwitz (aka Moe Howard)
Value of Property Stolen_____Value Recovered_____
```

Details of Complainant

Agnes Bojaxhiu witnessed a man with a bowl-shaped haircut beat a man with stringy hair senseless every time the stringy-haired man said the words "Niagara Falls." The stringy-haired man would stand up, brush himself off, confused as to why he had just been attacked, and then ask the assailant why it was that "Niagara Falls" set him off, only to set the man with the bowl-shaped haircut off again. This happened four or five times in quick succession, each episode ending with the stringy-haired man knocked to the ground. Agnes ascertained the names of both assailant and victim by asking a passerby.

```
                    Officers J B Winthrop____
                    Division    Patrol_____
                    Time 7:25 p.m. 10-5-29___
```

DOCUMENT #2

From the Desk of Moe Howard

January 3, 1972

Dear Pope Paul VI:

　　I don't want to be presumptuous, but maybe you've heard of me? Do Moe, Larry, and Curly ring a bell? What about Moe, Larry, and Shemp? Anyone ever say "nyuk, nyuk, nyuk" to you, your holiness? You ever get the Three Stooges on the boob tube over there? Well, I'm *that* Moe. That's right—the "two-fingers-poked-in-your-eyes" Moe. The "I'll-scrape-your-face-with-a-cheese-grater-if-need-be" Moe. The "my-hand's-stuck-in-a-flower-pot-so-I'll-break-it-over-your-head" Moe. For over forty years, I was the chief stooge. I was the angry one, the one who frowned and seethed at the same time. I should probably tell you something else up front. I'm a Jew. I say this so that all cards are on the table. No disrespect, sir, but my last name is Horwitz. My father was Solomon Horwitz and my mother was Jennie Gorovitz. We're a family of Levite and Lithuanian Jewish ancestry. So let's get one thing straight. I didn't kill Jesus Christ. And to the best of my knowledge, no Horwitz was involved. Okay? Are we clear on that? You see, when I was a kid, a bunch of Catholic kids beat the crap out of me and called me a Christ killer, and so I think now's a pretty good time to go on the record and say, "It wasn't me, buddy."

Anyway, here's the deal. I was just reading this book <u>Something Beautiful for God</u> by Malcolm Muggeridge (Muggeridge: some name, huh?), and it's all about one of your flock, a bride of Christ named Mother Teresa. I'm assuming you heard of her? Well, I saw Muggeridge's documentary on Mother Teresa, too, with the supposed divine light, but I talked to all the cameramen I ever worked with over the years, and they all assured me that the light was the result of some brand-new, never-before-used, high-speed Kodak film that was being used. Apparently, no other film stock was working for those lighting conditions, so Muggeridge's camera-crew decided to give this new Kodak stuff a whirl as a kind of last ditch effort. It was Muggeridge and Muggeridge alone who proclaimed that it was divine light. (Now, you tell me: Who among them has a vested interest in proving that this Mother Teresa gal was touched by God? Huh? It sure as hell doesn't hurt Muggeridge's book sales, now does it?)

All right. You may be scratching that tall pope hat of yours right about now and asking yourself, What does any of this have to do with Moe Howard? Well, listen, bub: It wasn't until I read Muggeridge's book and saw that Mother Teresa's name is really Agnes Bojaxhiu that I realized that I'd had my own little encounter with Big Mama T, oh, forty-some years ago. It was on the corner of 42nd and Broadway, and my brother Shemp and I had just finished a show. You see, Shemp and I, along with Larry Fine (another Jew, or so he claimed), were vaudevillians. (If you're a fan of the Stooges, your holiness, you may be asking yourself: Didn't Shemp come later? Didn't Curly come first? Well, yes and no. Not to bore you with all the little details, but...Shemp was one of the original Stooges, but he and this fellow we worked for, Ted Healy, they didn't get along so well, so Shemp left to begin his own career. That's when Curly stepped in. When we finally broke away from Ted for good and started making the famous two-reelers for Columbia Pictures that you're probably familiar with, Curly was our star stooge. Fourteen years later, Curly has a stroke, a bad one, and guess who we get to fill his shoes? Shemp, of course. And Shemp stayed with us for another nine years, until the day he died, God rest his soul.) Sorry for the tangent, but I didn't want you getting hung up on some trivial sidebar when the main issue, the reason I'm writing, is to let you know that your servant Mother Teresa isn't the gal you think she is!

The short version is this: Mother Teresa witnessed me and Shemp doing one of our acts on the street, an act in which the words "Niagara Falls" made me crazy, so much so that I beat the holy hell out of Shemp. Shemp, who plays the naïf, continues to say "Niagara Falls" and, in turn, continues to get beaten up. Mother Teresa - aka Agnes - apparently saw this and, with only a cursory knowledge of English and no knowledge whatsoever of vaudeville, filed a police report. The upshot is that I ended up in jail until Shemp could bail me out, but since Shemp had gone to Atlantic City (the poor guy's deadly sin was that he liked to gamble), I spent the weekend in the clink. When the manager of the theater learned that I'd been locked up, he suspended all us for a week until we convinced him that it had all been a misunderstanding. What I'm saying is this: Mother Teresa nearly ruined the Stooges. And since she disappeared right after the incident, I've never been afforded an opportunity to tell her precisely what she put us through.

You're probably asking yourself, So? Why should I care? I'm the Pope. I've got bigger fish to fry.

And you're right. You do. Except that I fear Muggeridge is going to push this woman toward sainthood or some such thing, and I'm here to tell you that she is far from being a saint. I wouldn't go so far as to say that she bears the mark of Satan or anything like that, but she's not who you think she is. And as for that beatific light that glowed behind her? You can thank technology for that, not God. Now, I've never seen the face of Jesus Christ on the belly of a toad, and I've never seen a statue of the Virgin Mary weeping (to wit: I'm a Jew), but please, I urge you, don't start confusing special effects for miracles, lest God becomes no different from Houdini, and the church becomes a burlesque hall. It's a slippery slope, my friend, and one that I would suggest you avoid if at all possible.

With the greatest respect,
Moe Howard

P.S. My wife, Helen, is Harry Houdini's cousin, so it's okay for me to make swipes at him like that.

DOCUMENT #3

From the Desk of Moe Howard

February 15, 1972

Dear Pope Paul VI:
    It's me…Moe. Hey, listen. I never heard back from you. Am I boring you? Am I taking up your valuable time?
    Inside this box you'll find a Bell and Howell 8 mm projector and a couple of my films. I've enclosed one film with Curly, A Pain in the Pullman, and one starring Shemp, Squareheads of the Round Table. I may have been presumptuous in my last letter to assume you were familiar with my work. Why would you be? Oh sure, I'm familiar with your work (and I'm familiar with your boss's work), but, hey, I'm just a Stooge. Even so, I don't think that's any reason not to respond to me. Therefore, I'm including a carbon copy of my last letter to you. I hope you'll take the time to watch these two films and respond to the concerns I have with Mother Teresa. If nothing else, I would very much appreciate it if you would at least acknowledge receipt of my letters and assure me that they will be placed in a special file in the event Mother Teresa is ever either beatified or canonized.
    In the meantime, I hope you enjoy the two short movies! I hand-picked them for you. A Pain in the Pullman features a pet monkey, and if there's one thing I've learned over the years, people love watching monkeys! Also: thought you might like the medieval setting of Squareheads of the Round Table.

All best,
Moe Howard

DOCUMENT #4

From the Desk of Moe Howard

March 18, 1972

Dear Pope:
   You don't want to correspond with me? Fine. But let me say this. Most people I know would have, at the very least, sent a thank you card for the projector and movies. Those weren't cheap gifts. Or maybe you watched the two movies and they weren't to your liking. Hey; whatever. Maybe you'd have preferred a print of Charleton Heston in <u>The Ten Commandments</u>? Too bad. Or maybe it's because I'm a Jew. Is that it? You don't commiserate with Jews? Okay; fine. I just taped a note to my fridge: No more gifts for the Pope!
   Good day, sir.

Deeply disappointed,
Moe Howard

DOCUMENT #5

From the Desk of Moe Howard

May 6, 1972

Dear Pope Paul VI:
   Boy, am I embarrassed! Of course I should have known how long packages take to ship overseas. That's just me, I guess…quick to offend! I suppose all those years of poking my friends in the eyes or hitting them with hammers and saw blades must have done something to my patience. Please forgive me.
   On another note, I'm pleased to hear how much you loved the two movies, especially <u>A Pain in the Pullman</u>. It's always been one of my favorites. I was sorry, though, that you didn't have much to say about Shemp or his performance in <u>Squareheads of the Round Table</u>. It's always been my belief that Shemp is underrated. I would never go so far as

to say that Curly is overrated; it's just that Shemp's performance as a Stooge has always been measured against Curly's, whom he replaced. (Remember, though: Shemp was an original Stooge and Curly replaced HIM first, and THEN Shemp replaced Curly many years later. I apologize if we've covered this ground before. It's just that so few people realize this fact.) Shemp had his own delivery, his own gags, his own distinct comic persona. He wasn't trying to imitate Curly, nor should he have.

But I digress. My main concern is that your letter made no mention of Mother Teresa, nothing about my complaint and/or concerns. Please don't sweep this under the rug. You won't be Pope forever – I'm sure this isn't news to you – and the last thing I would hate to see is a new Pope, a Pope unfamiliar with my charges against her, pick up Malcolm Muggeridge's torch, fabricated as it is, and take off running with it.

With respect and apologies,
Moe Howard

DOCUMENT #6

From the Desk of Moe Howard

April 23, 1972

Dear Pope Paul VI:

While I appreciate your letter extolling the virtues of Shemp and your apologies for the unintended slight, I'm very much worried that I derailed the point of my letter by spending far more time discussing the differences between my two brothers while bringing up the issue of Mother Teresa only at the very end of the discussion. Please, please acknowledge that you have at least read my complaint against this woman, and that you understand my worries. That's all I'm asking.

Yours,
Moe Howard

DOCUMENT #7

From the Desk of Moe Howard

November 8, 1972

Dear Pope Paul VI:
   Yes, of course I'll send a few more of our films. Enclosed you will find <u>Woman Haters</u> (our first two-reeler for Columbia), <u>You Nazty Spy!</u> (my personal favorite of all the Stooge shorts), <u>Hold That Lion!</u> (with Shemp but also featuring a cameo by Curly), and <u>Heavenly Daze</u> (a little something that might be up your alley). Again, no mention of Mom Teresa or Agnes or whatever alias she's using these days.

Curiously,
Moe Howard

DOCUMENT #8

From the Desk of Moe Howard

December 1, 1972

Dear P. P.:
   No, I will not send you any Laurel and Hardy movies. You can order those, if you're interested, from Blackhawk Films in Davenport, Iowa. You can find Charlie Chaplin movies there as well. Just write to them. I'm sure they would be happy to send a catalog to the Pope. And, no, I am not interested in flying to Rome, all expenses paid, to perform for you and the visiting Bishops on Christmas. I'm a seventy-one year old man. Those movies you are watching were made over thirty years ago. If you're so inclined, why don't you stage your own pie fight? Why do you need me? Poke each other in the eyes, if you're that hard-up for entertainment.

Nobody's clown,
Moe

DOCUMENT #9

From the Desk of Moe Howard

December 30, 1972

Dear Paul/6:
   Good question about why a bald man would be named Curly. It's a little something we here call IRONY!
   And so now I must ask you not to write to me anymore. Though I appreciate your newfound interest in slapstick, I can no longer continue this conversation until my concerns have been addressed.

With regrets,
Moe Howard

Editor's Note: According to the papal log-book, Pope Paul VI continued writing to Moe Howard until Moe's death on May 4, 1975 at the age of seventy-seven, but no one knows where these letters are or if they are still in existence. Pope Paul VI died August 6, 1978 at the age of eighty after a fifteen-year papacy. His successor was John Paul I, who died a little over a month after becoming pope. It was under Pope John Paul II that Mother Teresa finally received beatification. For the record, Pope John Paul II beatified 1,340 people—more than any previous pope.

The following (and final) document is a photocopy from Moe Howard's private diary which was recently purchased on eBay by a collector of Three Stooge memorabilia. This item did not come to light during James Tuttle's short life and is included here only to provide a larger, more complicated context for the documents that have already been provided. The date on the letter is the same date that Moe Howard was arrested for assault. Make of it what you will.

DOCUMENT #10

October 5, 1929
   Helen and I'd had a big fight this morning, an awful fight,

and she left for the week with little Joan to stay with friends. Later tonight, while talking to Shemp, I saw the most beautiful woman standing kitty-corner to us. This woman – no, no, more of a girl, really – she caught my eye. I can't say why exactly. She looked lost. She looked from another time, another place. I nudged Shemp and said, "Hey, let's do Niagara Falls," and he said, "Here? Now?" Shemp was tired, he'd just lit a cigarette, and only a half-hour earlier we'd finished our act. He wanted a drink (the guy drinks like a fish, I swear), and he was itching to get the hell away for the weekend, but I convinced him to do it, anyway. I waited until the girl across the street looked over and then I slammed into Shemp, as hard as I could, and Shemp said, "Watch where you're going, friend!" and I said, loud enough for her to hear me, "Friend! No one's called me 'friend' in years!" and a crowd started to gather, a few of whom knew us, most of whom didn't, and I kept hoping that this beautiful, wraithlike girl would cross the street, but she stayed where she was, rooted to her corner, and so I continued on, beating Shemp mercilessly, as if possessed by the devil himself, but occasionally looking over at her, across the street, grinning like a maniac, sometimes winking, hoping to lure her over... but for what, I wondered? Was she an angel, or had she been sent here to test me? I don't know. I don't know, and I should be glad I never found out. And yet... I wish I at least knew her name. I wish I knew her name, and why a light, as bright as any I'd ever seen, seemed to shine from behind her. It kills me to think I'll never know answers to the simplest of questions.

Michael Garriga

EMILE GRIFFITH AND MUHAMMAD ALI
INHABIT THE BODIES OF THE LAST ROOSTERS TO LEGALLY FIGHT IN LOUISIANA, AUGUST 15, 2008

Caesar Julius

WHITEHACKLE
Weight: 4:02
Age: 29 months
Record: 8-0

A peace stills the certain center of me when he takes my beak inside his mouth, rubs my fluff feathers, and settles the jerking muscles along my spine—he does not call me chanticleer nor the vile cock, but rather Caesar, always Caesar, with a noble flourish, cooing with his sweet hands on me. Even when they dubbed my wattle and comb, his look calmed me. His eyes focus my attention, save me from all distraction: the pick-ups eaten by rust and rent with neglect, the old man pushing the wheelbarrow filled with ice water and cans of beer,

I Am

O'NEAL RED
Weight: 4:07
Age: 26 months
Record: 6-0

Me rooster strut daddy, me señor cock of the walk, gotta prick longer than yo' talon gaff—and look at this *maricón*, this capon, they've brought me to slay, too lazy to learn his proper pecking order place. I put him just above these sad ass men who've come to see the rooster snuft again, but ain't brought enough fire to kill me, see it in they eyes, and this bird's too—his cooing eyes cooing that cock handler's—but what's a man to me but a builder of fences and cages, while I am free with skill enough to holler the Sun, and the Sun know

(Caesar Julius, continued.)

shouting above the other shouts of men with knives and cash pushed at each other, the smells of turpentine and sawdust, whiskey and tobacco. So I'll crow from the mountain tops: I love my man more than my hens—shameful to some, I know, like this rooster strutting across from me, contempt nested there in his eyes, yet in these last still moments before combat I can't help myself: I slip into thoughts of his hands on my back cape, stroking my neck, and the solemn way he takes the leather straps and wets them and fastens the razor-gaffs to my spur stumps, and runs his thumb nails up the ridges of my shank, and sometimes I feign fevered exhaustion so he'll spit into my mouth, almost, but never quite, quenching my thirst—and for his affections I have become lethal, killing again and again. And though I hate the spurting gore I cause, my fellow birds bleeding their lives out for me, I'd bathe gladly preening in their guts for the joy it brings my man—and this puffed up Bantam across from me will be no different: steady me, Sun, and forgive me please my unnatural love, but I will have my man crow once more, "Caesar! Caesar!"

(I Am, continued.)

better than not rise when I peck and call. Because I am the greatest. Been blessed with this chest, swollen and strong as any Bantam you ever saw, and when asked why fight, I say, Why not? I am hot like July sand, like god don't give a damn, and it ain't nothing but a thang for me to survey my land perched ten feet off the ground, while empty-headed chicken heads empty they eggs into my nests. And I am still here because I say you ain't, and because I say it, boy, you ain't. I Am. Bowed up and just so purty, watch how I dance my cockerel-waltz now. And when you call me fighter, I correct, and say killer: four pounds of fury ready for any round robin, rounding up robins and bobbin' jays straying too close to the road, keepin' them fox and snake at bay. And you, you needs to pray, Little One, for the odd chance to find any one of my tail feathers fallen, use it as a talisman to conjure the devil, and when you do, ask him for me: Which came first, Old Scratch, the chicken or the egg? And that old timer will tell you every time, "That bad ass bird, I Am!" I Am.

Peleas de Gallo:
Hector Velazquez, 32, Caesar Julius's Cocker,
Pumpkin Center, LA, August 15, 2008

We release the birds, and it is beautiful this dance, this violent pirouette, highstep and prance, all gay color, bright plume, and kicks, and through the slash and slash of the gaffs, which strobe the lights above, I see the cop with gun and stick, and he looks much like the man who took my big brother away after he stabbed the jefe in that *Pontchatoula* strawberry field—that no paying liar who made a slave of us both—stabbed him as Caesar now stabs his foe, the bird falling and turning away, Caesar's blade caught in the bird's chicken heart, and we rush into the gallodrome to separate them, and I hold Caesar while the other cocker slips the gaff out his bird, whose blood bursts and throbs and throbs the more, his life only worth the making of small mud puddles in the sawdust and dirt, and the police is in the ring too, pushing us both away from our birds, his hand is on my chest and I think how if tomorrow we bring our cocks to fight—a thing which is true to their own fowl nature—he'd arrest me, send me home to Guadalajara or to jail, one more place like a pen where my brother spent his last years, having to stick and stab to stay alive, a pen like Caesar has never known, and now I hear a loud ruckus behind me, a clanging on the bleachers, a metallic roaring in this insulated barn, these men with so much money to win and lose press in on me—these cracker and coonass and cowboy alike—have crowded in against me to see which dead bird has become dead bird first, and they are hollering threats and bargains, and I am surrounded, outnumbered as always here, their hands and heat upon me, and Caesar's blood coats my hand, the other bird's gaff is lodged in his neck, the two joined forever in life and death, and the smell of diesel from the generators suddenly makes me go woozy, sweat pouring down my back, and I look up and try to inhale fresh air, the strings of light like banners above in the rafters, and shouts rising like rapture, like the hair on my neck, and there is a mass screaming and groaning, and I look down and my bird's eyes have gone from glass to gravy, but he has lived the longest, and his eyes are like mine, misty, and I scream, "Caesar! Goddamnit, Caesar!" and I reach for him again but the policia stop me again with his stick this time as they stopped mi hermano in jail with stick after stick until the final stick they stuck in his arm sent him to his long home rest, and so I reach into my penche pantspocket to be cooled by the steel of my switchblade and pray for the rare courage of my brother and Caesar, to strike as mi hermano and this brave bird, mi hermanito, both did: to stab and stick, to kill and die.

Margaret McMullan

WRESTLING WITH ANDY KAUFMAN

non-fiction

I was working as an assistant entertainment editor for *Glamour* magazine in New York. A publicist called to pitch a bizarre play involving Deborah Harry and Andy Kaufman wrestling. My editor didn't think our readers would be interested in wrestling, but they were interested in knowing what "Blondie" was doing. She told me to "check out" the rehearsals during my lunch hour.

This was April 1983. Ronald Reagan was President. This was the year Karen Carpenter died of not eating and Tennessee Williams died choking on an aspirin cap. We were all dancing at discos to "Beat It."

When I saw that the stage was a wrestling ring meant to look like one in Atlantic City, I knew I'd never write about it, not for *Glamour*. I sat in a bleacher-style seat, one seat away from Deborah Harry who had a white towel around her neck even though she wasn't sweating. She was no longer the blond of Blondie. She was fat and she had red hair and she got up to move around the ring with Andy Kaufman. This was her Broadway debut. Andy wore white leggings, baggy shorts, and a white t-shirt. He had a big belly. They both wore wrestling shoes and acted ridiculously intense. I was twenty-three years old and knew very little about the entertainment world, but my first thought was, Why are these two famous people ruining their careers with wrestling? They couldn't think of anything else?

They weren't on stage for long. Deborah Harry sat back down near me, but not next to me. I told her my name and the magazine I was with and she got up and moved. She told her publicist she didn't want to meet me.

I had only been working at *Glamour* for one year, but I had been turned down before. Alice Walker hung up on me because she said she had better things to do then to answer questions for *Glamour.* I tended to have more respect for the ones who refused interviews. I watched Deborah Harry's still beautiful, pale white profile as she yelled at her publicist. We would run the story we already had on The Pretenders or Joan Jett or someone else, after all. Even I knew then that this play would fail.

Andy sat down next to me. Maybe he saw that I had a tape recorder and that I was writing things in a notepad. Maybe he saw me and liked me. Maybe he felt sorry for me. Maybe he overheard, *Glamour*, and thought, well now I wouldn't mind being in there.

I know enough about people now to know that you never really know them. Not really. But we writers are told early on to write what we know about who we know. So how do you write about the people we've known, knowing what we know and what we don't know? And how do you write about people who may not wish to be written about?

Like some writers working from memory, I often struggle to get the facts and the people right. One mistake turns it into fiction. I want to remember everything that happened as it happened with Andy, and I want to consider the effects.

We talked. I can't remember what we talked about but I remember laughing. I remember thinking I should be appreciating this moment more because it wasn't an interview. I dated men in college who had a bizarre adoration for Andy Kaufman. They would drink and do imitations of Andy doing imitations of the Eastern block immigrants he did on "Saturday Night Live." I never thought it was funny when they did it. But there I was in the bleacher seats laughing. He kept playing with tone. That I remember. At first, it wasn't *what* he said, but *how* he said it, and then he would turn the formula. He said something ridiculous all serious, no smiles and I tried very hard to best him. I was that naïve.

He challenged me to a wrestling match. Not on stage, but privately, back stage, behind the bleachers, not in front of anyone. He was the one who pointed out that I was wearing a dress. It was a blue cotton dress with a drop waist and pink flowers. It was all wrong, but I loved that dress. I did not feel wrong in that dress. I felt very much right. I even wore pink lipstick I'd gotten from Beauty to match the little pink flowers.

I met Keith Richards and danced with Mick Jagger at Tavern on the Green in this dress. Ron Wood said that I was a "smily little bird" in this dress. It had become my good luck dress. It was one of the few dresses I could afford. I had two suits and this one dress. I wore the dress to one of my first screenings of "The Day After," a TV movie about the effects of a nuclear strike on a U.S. town. It was a comfortable dress I could wear to work, then go out in afterwards. I lived in a studio apartment six flights up, no elevator, and the only time I went home was to sleep in a fold-out sofa bed.

I still had a perm then too, and my hair was rag-tag wild in a Tina Turner way, which was really my styling method of avoiding a Manhattan haircut for which I had neither the time nor the money.

He asked me if I had it turned on. He was referring to the tape recorder, though he didn't make a big deal about double meanings. Or maybe I had turned it on, and he asked me if it was on. I know it was on, because it recorded everything, and I know this because afterwards I played it all back, then later, when I quit my job at *Glamour* I stared at those mini-tapes marked Andy Kaufman for the longest time, wanting to take them, but leaving them in the end because I had been on the job, so they inevitably belonged to Condé Nast.

We went behind the bleacher seats. No one saw us. The staff and crew were busy packing up and talking about the ridiculous play. I know now that this was the juncture in time when Andy was desperately trying to revive his career.

He spread out a blue mat on the floor. He told me to take my shoes off and I did. I was young. I had nothing to lose. That month, a bomb planted by Shiite Muslims had destroyed the U.S. Embassy in Beirut. Reagan backed Contra rebels in Nicaragua. Millions were dying in Ethiopia from the two-year drought. Rock stars sang for them. In my mind, at that point in time, the worst thing that could happen to anybody usually happened in other countries.

I had on my lucky dress. I know I thought about what I wore underneath the lucky dress too. Before I left for New York, my college roommate and I went to a going-out-of-business sale at a lingerie shop in Grinnell, Iowa. I loaded up on garters from the 1950s and silk stockings that came folded in beautiful beige boxes. I was wearing these when I wrestled with Andy.

I pinned him midway. It wasn't easy, but it wasn't difficult either. This was before I ever heard about weights or really "working out." Every now and then I ran or swam. But I was young. I didn't have to do anything with regularity. Not even boyfriends.

Of course he could have been faking it all. I knew that then and I know that now.

This is when I should step forward and say everyone has a past. Everyone has had a life different than the life she lives now. This was before literature changed my life. The beauty, the life-changing aspect of reading literature, especially American literature, is to read and to become acquainted with characters who are capable of change, and discovering people who can actually remake themselves. Currently, I am a happily married woman with a son and a dog. I am also a professor at a university. I was neither married nor any sort of teacher in 1983.

I straddled him, holding him by his wrists for a long time. Did I say I had nothing to lose? Did I say I was very young? He had the belly, a high belly, so the straddling was difficult. I inched more towards his chest, thinking, knowing, that to inch the other way would be dangerous. Dangerous? There I was in my dress, in my garters, straddling Andy Kaufman, pinning his hands to the mat, saying, "I win." This is what happened. What happened happened. But what was the effect?

He asked if the recorder was on. I said yes. He reached over and turned it off. Latoya Jackson did this once, and made me erase everything that she and her mother had said which was not much. So I laughed at Andy—laughed!—and I reached over and turned the recorder back on. I rolled off of him then; I do remember that because when I let go and he lifted his hands from the mat, he put them on my waist in the nicest way, to help land me from his belly as though to fall would be equivalent to a tumble off Mount Everest.

He said I had to promise I wouldn't tell anyone about this. He made me promise. He was doing that tone thing again, but this time, I really couldn't tell if he was joking or not. You have to promise. If it got out, he said. If people knew, he said. I think I owe you money now, he said. And I did, I promised I wouldn't tell, but I was still laughing.

Out of the blue, that same week, Andy came to my office in the Condé Nast building on Madison Avenue in Midtown Manhattan wearing cut-off shorts, a Hawaiian shirt, and a crochet hat he said he stole off a black "dude" in Harlem. Of course, he had to have known what he was doing, going into the building where he'd be riding elevators with models and editors for *GQ, Vogue,* and *Vanity Fair*. Betty, our receptionist, was tickled and giggly—this from a woman who put a big red hibiscus flower behind her ear every morning to answer phones. She personally walked Andy to my office, introducing his presence with great flourish, giggling all the while even though he didn't say a word.

He wanted a tour, which I gave him, but he stopped short midway down the hall, somewhere between Research and Beauty. He looked pale. He said he didn't want to meet anyone and he stuck his head inside my over-sized bag. I don't know now why I had the bag with me. Perhaps because I expected to go to lunch with him. But I remember clearly that he stuck his head inside the bag because it was such a bizarre, hilarious and intimate thing to do. I read recently that women unconsciously consider their handbags extensions of their bodies, so that when a woman, say, pets her purse while talking to a man, the man can assume she is being flirtatious. I think nothing of handbags, but I knew even then, that when a man—comedian or otherwise—sticks his head inside the bag I'm holding, it means *something*. It certainly had an effect.

He said he had come by to take me to tea. He had a cold and a cough and he was fasting. He said he was purifying himself. A Yogi in L.A. taught him to fast flues out. But he could have tea. He knew of a place. My boss had not come in that day and wasn't there to say I could not go to lunch. I don't recall even hesitating to go.

I assumed I was being used and I assumed he thought he was being used too. I would attempt to pitch a story about him or about his projects. Meanwhile, I would get to hang out and be seen with Andy Kaufman, except that very few people in New York recognized him at that time.

We took a cab downtown, then we sat at a table at EAT. The overhead fans were going. We used the restaurant's crayons and doodled on the white paper tablecloth as we talked. I think I ordered a muffin, while he drank pots of herbal tea. He was only drinking tea, he said. He said he looked me up in the phone book. He called and called. He said he wanted me to go out with him. He wanted to know why I didn't have an answering machine. Answering machines were relatively new at that time and I told him that when I wasn't home I wasn't home, end of story. The fact was I couldn't afford an answering machine. If people called, they called me at work where I sat behind a desk most of the time wearing my blue dress.

We talked about yoga and concentration, what focus really meant, and out of nowhere, in an angry way, he asked me what I was doing there.

Drinking tea with you, I said, startled and even a little scared.

No, he said. He wanted to know what the hell I was doing in New York. I told him I was working at this job that was considered a dream job by so many. My editor was in fact in the habit of standing before me and asking me if I knew how lucky I was to have the job I had because there were so many other girls who wanted it. I may have told him this too.

But it's not a dream job, not to you. He said that or something very much like that.

I know now that he was sick then and that he knew about the cancer. And I know now that he didn't tell many people and that later, when he did tell, very few believed him. They thought his "sick act" was another performance piece. Was the illness or the treatment wreaking havoc on his moods when I met him? Not long after that I would read in Page Six that he beat up a photographer, or was it a fan? His anger came quickly and out of nowhere, I could see that. Still, I wonder what Andy saw that day, and what he thought about me, a comparative stranger. He didn't know me and I didn't know him, only of him. But there was something, wasn't there? Something that we *did* know about each other?

That was the year you could fly from New York to London round-trip for $150 on People's Express. Meanwhile, I stayed holed up most of the time at the office, rotating my one dress and two suits.

Now of course, I think I see it. He was sick then, and he was looking for something, cures and comfort. Or maybe he just thought I needed company. For even though it looked it, I was not really in the right place at the right time. Not for me anyway. I had not formed many close friendships since I had moved to New York. I saw that the people I worked with all lived in "units" similar to my cage called a studio apartment, and that we were all living and breathing our jobs, and our jobs had become who we were and we had become our jobs.

He was living with his father at the time and his mother had been very sick. At least that's what he said. He said he and his parents were getting close again and he was glad for that and for this in between time. I remember thinking that we had slid into what I considered an earnest conversation. No jokes, no tone thing. Just two people having tea—nervous, doodling, talking. I wish I had saved the doodles.

In the 1999 movie "Man on the Moon," Jim Carrey playing Andy Kaufman says to Courtney Love playing Andy's girlfriend, "You don't know the real me."

"There isn't a real you," she says.

"Oh yeah," he says. "I forgot."

I know now that he had a girlfriend then, but I did not know that then and he never mentioned anyone else. I liked Andy, liked figuring out his brand of comedy, the story-telling without ever really having a punch line. On a separate occasion, Bill Murray came to the office—and he too wore a hairnet. He had good fun, joshing with my editor and with me. He and my editor graduated from the same high school in a northern suburb of Chicago. He played her, not by changing his voice, but by asking her questions about her accessories, and she laughed even though she could have just as easily been insulted. His tone was clear. You knew exactly when Murray was serious and when he was joking. Not many gray areas, which made his comedy easy.

Andy was all gray.

With fourteen previews, "Teaneck Tanzi: the Venus Flytrap" opened at The Nederlander Theater on a matinee and closed after the evening performance.

Frank Rich of *The New York Times* wrote:

The other source of amusement is one of the ushers. Slipped in among the bona fide employees of the Nederlander is a ringer - the comic Andy Kaufman. Mr. Kaufman's shtick, as his fans know, is hostility, and here he is, in the highest of dudgeon, a cigarette dangling from his lips, barking at seated customers. He demands to see our ticket stubs, and, should we not immediately locate them, he loudly threatens to eject us clear out to the street. As most of Mr. Kaufman's victims don't recognize him, there's sadistic fun to be had in watching the surly comedian provoke the uninitiated into angry screaming. A critic near me almost slugged him.

As it turned out, that may have been the high point of that critic's evening; it certainly was of mine. "Teaneck Tanzi" is an Americanized, retitled version of London's biggest comedy hit since "Steaming," and its charm must have bailed out somewhere over the Atlantic. What we find at the Nederlander is a theatrical gimmick whose execution produces a pounding sensation in every part of one's head except the brain.

Rich went on to write that Deborah Harry and Scott Renderer "make a worthwhile contribution by slurring some of their lines."

Andy called me at work shortly after the review came out. Neither of us mentioned it. I think maybe all his calls came to me at work, but I also recall at least one conversation when I was at home, because I remember staring at my blue phone, trying to picture what kind of phone he was talking into, making such mundane things funny.

We talked a great deal by phone which I felt was too much like work, but I think such relationships, if you can call them that, must be common because they are so easy. We talked on the phone most of all. We went out some. He liked to hold my hand.

A married friend of mine told me once that he had an affair with a married woman, and when she died, he said he did not go to her funeral because he said he could not. "Who was I?" he said over and over. "Who was I to attend her funeral?"

When I read in the paper that Andy died, I did not go to his funeral in Great Neck, New York where over 300 family and friends gathered. I sat down at my desk in my office to write something about him, but it came out all wrong. Here were the events, but what was the effect? I didn't know yet, of course. I was still deep in whatever was my life then. I remember reading—or did I overhear?—what somebody said about the funeral. He kept thinking that Andy was going to pop out of his coffin. I heard that friends even poked at his body to see if this was one more performance stunt. And really, he was so good at what he did, who could blame them?

I stayed on in New York for one more year. Andy died in May, and one weekend in June, I rode my bike to upstate New York and happened upon the house where Barbara McClintock lived and grew corn that earned her a Nobel Prize for her contributions to genetics. Every minute I was working or thinking of working, but this time I paused just to marvel at Barbara McClintock's corn. During the one vacation I took in three years, I excused myself during dinner to call Sally Ride to interview her about her experiences on the Challenger. She told me what it was like to see earth from so far away, near the moon, and again, I marveled at the view she described, wondering about my own direction. Standing in that phone booth during my vacation, I thought hard about what Andy had said: What the hell are you *doing* here?

It's hard to know a person, hard to know what a person did or did not mean.

I want so badly to get this right.

He walked me home once. Or did we take a cab? I remember standing on the steps. Lynn Fontanne died that year. She and her husband lived in a house in Wisconsin that had a lot of steps. Her husband said that stairs were wonderful for entrances and exits and lovemaking.

Andy stood on the bottom step. I stood on the step above. He held my hand. He had small, pale hands with bits of dark hair on the knuckles. He had sweet, close-together eyes, long lashes, and the eyebrows of course, the eyebrows that mingled together, connecting without quite altogether meeting.

"No memoirist writes for long without experiencing an unsettling disbelief about the reliability of memory, a hunch that memory is not, after all, just memory," Patricia Hampl writes in *I Could Tell You Stories*. "Memoir is a peculiarly open form, inviting broken and incomplete images, half-recollected fragments, all the mess of detail."

Memory is such a strange mix of recall and taking apart what is recalled if only just to rethink the event through one more time.

There was no way I was going to sleep with him.

I kissed him goodnight. The effect of the kiss did not move me, and I don't think it did anything for him either, but still, he did not want to leave. This was when he was sick. This was right before he left New York for the last time. I thought of the mess in my unit of a cage six flights up—the pulled out sofa bed, the army of cockroaches that scattered not when the door opened, but leisurely now, after I had moved about the room. They were that comfortable in my place now. That place was no place for guests.

I regret that I didn't have the moxy or the energy to head for a bar and stay up all night in order to sit and talk with Andy. But I do remember I just didn't want to and I don't think he did either.

He said then that he was going somewhere, on a trip, to the Philippines perhaps, and that I should think about going with him. He said I didn't belong in Manhattan. In my mind, I remember thinking, how would you know where I belong? You don't know me, not really. His tone was gentle and serious. He looked me in the eye as he spoke. He was thirty-four years old and he had one year left to live.

I write now, not about what I know, but about what I want to know.

"I persist in believing the event has value," Hampl writes. "Stalking the relationship, seeking the congruence between stored image and hidden emotion—that's the real job of memoir."

In my mind, I see him so clearly. There he is in a hair net, shorts and the Hawaiian shirt. I can't recall the colors, but I know yellow and red were involved. Do I say that because those are my son's favorite colors?

He's come to take me to tea.

John Flaherty

THE 103RD STORY
OR
HOW MURPH JR. BEATS MURPH TO THE TOP OF THE SEARS TOWER

> *Does one climb a glass mountain, at considerable personal discomfort, simply to disenchant a symbol?*
> —Donald Barthelme, "The Glass Mountain"

1. I am racing my Dad to the top of the Skydeck on the 103rd story of the Sears Tower.
2. He is the three-time reigning champion of the *Go Vertical Chicago* annual stair-climbing competition.
3. The organizers release racers in packs of ten at thirty-second intervals and I am pushing my way through the pack to the fourth floor.
4. When I open up toward the fifth, some waste-of-space weekend warrior's Reeboked heel bats my balls.
5. But I don't even feel it—that's how locked in I am.
6. I will catch my Dad, whose group went first and who has a two-minute headstart.
7. Mid-stride my elbow connects with a fish fin—or a chick's ear—as I blow by early stragglers from the pack released thirty seconds ahead of me.
8. I am going to beat Old Murph and his record-setting time of 13 minutes and 24 seconds.
9. 13 minutes and 24 seconds to a finish line 1,353 feet above the ground.
10. That is a sick time.
11. Especially for a sixty-year-old man.
12. Who in his life has never stepped into a gym.

13. This stairwell smells worse than a gym: each step a potpourri of ass, feet and baby powder.
14. "Pushup and situps," Dad would say out back of our brick bungalow in West Lawn. "Save that Nautilus-Total-Gym bullshit for your sister."
15. But I do not have a sister.
16. Never did.
17. Mom died when I was five.
18. Murphy House was a Sausage Fest: just Dad, me, and two little brothers too chickenshit to enter this race.
19. Robbie and Stevie both afraid of the Old Man who thinks of everything as a competition.
20. Like with food: each of his workweek "Big Man" turkey sandwiches weigh four pounds.
21. Or with beer: Lite-shit is pussy shit.
22. And most definitely with work: a real job—one a man could be proud of—is pushing a mower for his landscaping company twelve hours a summer day—without breaks: you ate in the car between jobs.
23. Hell, with him, even the old "having-a-catch" was jacked up to me, him, Rob, Steve on the front lawn in an every-man-for-himself game of Smear the Queer.
24. But I have been training for three months now.
25. I am at the 25th floor and I am flying.
26. I keep my elbows tight to my body and try to keep my upper body loose.
27. I focus on breathing.
28. I drive through each step.
29. I push off each landing to take two steps.
30. Training started when I moved my family into a highrise 27 floors above the Gold Coast.
31. When I signed a mortgage on the place, William—the son who I did not name Joseph Aloisius Murphy III—was a week old and Tara—the wife—freaked.
32. But every time Baby William needed diapers or Tara needed Reese's Peanut Butter Cups—her stress-reliever of choice since

college—I ran down the 27 flights to Gufran's overpriced corner store on Division & Clarke.
33. Then I ran back up.
34. Same deal at work.
35. Thirty-three stories up.
36. Thirty-three stories down.
37. First day I got into the AON building's stairwell and tried climbing 300 feet to my classy cubicle at Bucci, Baker & Copeland, I made it to just the fourth floor.
38. I was wearing my suit.
39. Daryl, AON's no-bullshit security guard, was pointing a gun in my face.
40. It was a loaded M-9 9mm Beretta pistol he kept from the Army.
41. I wiped a little sweat from my lip and said, "We cool?"
42. "Fuck, Joe. Unless you a firefighter, a terrorist or a motherfucking rat—keep your lawyering ass out a them stairways."
43. I am a third of the way to the Skydeck and I am running at four minutes.
44. Daryl and I worked out our misunderstanding with some Bears tickets and I kept training at work.
45. But work and home weren't enough.
46. I donated $1000 to Save Sick Kids and raced last-minute in *Hustle Up the Hancock*.
47. I got up its 96 floors and its 1632 steps in 36 minutes and 43 seconds.
48. But it wasn't enough training and I didn't have enough time before Dad's race.
49. So I flew to Taiwan for the only stair-climbing race I could find.
50. I spent $2300 on a United Airlines coach ticket.
51. I called in favors from Duchovny Davis—a former Georgetown roommate and a current U.S. State Department agent—to get me an emergency travel visa.
52. Duchovny owed me.
53. But he didn't seem to think so.
54. So I blackmailed him.
55. Wild Turkey + scuba masks + grape Jell-O + tiny-sized foreign

exchange students + bookcases of drugs + an unexpected-Murph Jr. coming back to his dorm early from Thanksgiving Break
56. = public service career killer.
57. And I have photos.
58. And he wants to be a Senator.
59. The *Taipei 101 Run-Up* entry fee cost another two-grand.
60. The Chinese are sneaky fuckers.
61. For real: when I got to the top of the tower—that one that looks like bamboo—I had bruises and welts up and down my body from the other climbers' knees, elbows, feet and fists.
62. I looked like I had chewed gum, spat it at a picture of Chairman Mao, then gotten caned like a '60s Catholic schools kid.
63. But those Chinese know how to compete.
64. Over half-way to the top and now I feel my calf muscles tightening.
65. I feel each sinew of burning thigh muscle.
66. Each molecule of protein.
67. Every amino acid.
68. The marrow in my bones.
69. And each and every last drop of Chinese HGH that I injected into my ass before the race.
70. In Taiwan, after the run-up, in a hotel bar, with bags of ice taped to my legs underneath track pants, Lui Xiang—the Olympic hurdler and Coca-Cola spokesman—bought me a drink and explained how Americans misunderstand performance-enhancing drugs.
71. I have not seen another racer in four or five flights.
72. I check my watch: I am on pace.
73. Everything in the stairwell looks the same: gray, tough, and damp.
74. Only the numbers on each landing change.
75. They're getting bigger—larger—but then I have to check.
76. I am on 76.
77. Now 77.
78. So
79. why
80. are
81. people
82. going

How Murph Jr. Beats Murph to the Top of the Sears Tower

83. down
84. the
85. tower?
86. I keep pushing to the top, and see a flash of a red, black and white basketball uniform on a guy racing to the lower levels.
87. At the railing I pause—for a split-second—and he pauses before flashing me a big white smile that beams nearly as bright as his gold hoop earrings.
88. It's Michael Jordan.
89. I hear sneaker squeaks below me and hope it's just MJ's kicks and not some other climber coming up on me.
90. More people rush down the tower.
91. These others are not as fast nor as charismatic as Jordan—the God of Chicago—so I have more of a chance to see their faces.
92. Al Capone, the first Mayor Daley, Harry Caray, Ditka, Jane Adams, Marshall Field, Cyrus McCormick, Daniel Burnham, Louis Armour, Louis Sullivan, Mrs. O'Leary's Cow: they all are booking their shit toward the bottom of the tower.
93. I have ten flights to go and am on pace to break Dad—to break his record.
94. Half-a-story up I see the bottoms of Dad's gray worn Nikes.
95. At this point, with eight stories to go, I would have to collapse-down-dead to lose.
96. He would probably bury me under his shitty tomato plants in our West Lawn backyard.
97. He has refused to move on—to move forward—and insists on staying in the same shitty bungalow in the same shitty neighborhood.
98. I am yelling—screaming—something, as I slap up at his ankle.
99. He slips and I cut inside of him to grab the railing.
100. It's still wet with his sweat.
101. I pull myself higher and can hear cheering from up above.
102. I smell burning metal and exhaust; I worry the floors are mislabeled.

The Skydeck is under construction. I look up to see an atrium of steel paths that spiral endlessly into the sky. Construction workers—dudes in hard hats and tool belts—scurry up the elevating framework as they hammer and weld. Higher up the sun reflects off their gear and they look like stars. Without looking behind me, I run up after them.

El Pollo Diablo

THEODORE ROOSEVELT VS. SPRING HEELED JACK:
An Interviewings by Me, El Pollo Diablo, Dead Pirate from the Netherworld

When I was first asked to interview two great antagonistses, I balked at the idea. Firstlys, what great antagonists would be willing to sit in a rooms together in a peaceable natures, and secondlys who would be fools enough to sit in the room *with* them? Apparently, I is that fools. So that was one problem down. Then came the matter of who the subjects would be: Hannibal and Scipio? Oliver Cromwell and Ireland? Tipper Gore and Larry Flynt? Yes, there was many big choices to be made.

Finally I decided my minds up on focusing on a rather obscure legend of two great foes, who, as the story goes, battled for… well, if not humanity, at least for human dignity.

Spring Heeled Jack was a pestilence to Victorian era Great Britain, causing many terrors and ripped ladies' garments. Disappearing from the public scene for some times, then popping back up, Jack kept his legend going strongs for nearly four decades or more. It was not until the intervention of a young American upstart was Jack's reign of inconvenience slowed to a level of acceptablenesses.

At first it was difficult getting Spring Heeled Jack to agree to this interviewings, especially since he is, if nothing else, a creatures of ego, which is obvious upon first viewings of him in his bright red cape and shiny helmet. As I learned for myselfs, laughter at this outfit does not help you become his friends. He gets very angry, and his already thick Cockney accent becomes nearly indecipherables. And of course it is very hard to get him to regain his sittings to continues with any questions.

Once again, Jack, I apologizes for that. You just looked so precious in your little suit.

Now I presents to you an interview with two personages who, as legend has it, has shaped the destinys of the free world.

El Pollo Diablo: Firstlys, thank you for being here. I know that there is still some tensions in the air. My goal is not to re-open old woundings, but to educate the public on an important chapters of history.

Colonel Theodore Roosevelt: It is a pleasure to be here. An esteemed pleasure. I hold no animosity towards Mr. Jack. All of that was a long time ago, and as I learned from my father, the quality of a man lies in his ability to forgive his detractors while still standing up for his own principles.

Spring Heeled Jack: See here, you two. I'm a trans-dimensional being, see? *Trans- dimensional.* Wot that means, see, is that I got this ability here to jump from your world to mine. Zip! Zap! Zam! Here I is! Zoop! No I isn't! Now I's gone! So I's special, see? So I deserves me some respec.

EPD: Okay...

SHJ: Right Ted? Ted. Teddy. Teddy Ted Ted. You hate bein' called Ted, don't you?

TR: No, I really don't prefer...

SHJ: That's right you don't, Ted. Ted. You don't like it, Ted, and don't you forget it.

TR: That's just...

SHJ: Ted.

EPD: Let me address this first question to Mr. Jack. Being a trans-dimensional beings, as you puts it, what first brought you to the Earthly realm? Were you just out on a walks or...

SHJ: Nah. I was prayed here, see? Several hundred years ago, yeah? Them Central American blokes, see? Them was cutting out some hearts and chanting to bejesus for some rain or something, then quick as a wink on a fox with Tourette's, there I is. One minute I was chatting with the lads, then boffo! I's on top of some big stone thingy getting blood on me boots. An' wot kind of a greeting is that, I ask you? Gettin' blood on me boots. I gave them a what-for, believe you me.

EPD: So your first exposures to Earth was not in England at all. It was in Mesoamerica. I imagine your red eyes must have given them quite a frights.
SHJ: That ain't the half of it, mate. In case you ain't knowed this before, I'm a fire spitter.
TR: That's true. He definitely has the ability to breath fire. Why, when we had our very first brannigan…
SHJ: Right, Ted, who asked you?
TR: Manners, sir, manners.
SHJ: Anyways, I flashes me red eyes at 'em, see? Then I burns some of them fancy feathers and jaguar skins they was wearin' with a few belches of the ol' flameroo, an' I gots them heatherns eatin' out of me hands. An' wot with your puny gravity here I can leap buildings in a single bound, I can. That really made 'em jabber. So you name it, an' they was pilin' it at me feet. Gold. Cocoa beans. Yams. It was all me very own for the takin'.
EPD: So you helped bring them rains?
SHJ: Rain? 'Ell no. Wot do I look like? A bleedin' weather… bringer?
EPD: So what dids they do when you did not bring forths with the waters?
SHJ: Wot could they do? I just told 'em that I was pissed off, see? An' that they was going to have a long ways to go to make things square, yeah? An' what I really wanted was women. "Bring me your women!" I says to 'em.
TR: This is ridiculous! I did not come here to listen to some side-show braggadocio relive his exploits in Central America. Besides, if it's tales of the jungle you want, I have a few of my own. Like when I all but died in the jungles of the mighty Amazon. Why, there was this…
EPD: You is quite corrects. We should moves on. To save some time, let's jump to the forwards in history a little bits. Jack you left that dimension of Earth not long after you was caught diddling the daughter of the High Priest of Huitzilopochtli, is that not correct?
SHJ: Ah that bloke was pissed, yeah? So's I had to scarper, yeah? So's I moved from place to place, takin' in the local scenery an' whatnot. Eventually I done popped into London. Smokey place, that.
EPD: You apparently caused many a fusses.
SHJ: That I did mate. That I did. Like there's any harm trying to play a bit of tickle and squeal with the ladies. An' all that wailing about and

fainting they did. There was no call for all of that mess. Not wot I would call hospitable by a long shot.
EPD: And you just hanged about the place for eighty years or so?
SHJ: Come and go, yeah. Every so often I had to make me an appearance to keep me image up. Plus I had an inside deal with one of the local papers, see? Every once in a while I breath a little fire, rip me a bodice or two, leap from rooftop to rooftop… They sell more copy, an' I get a cut, yeah? Pretty plum deal, that.
EPD: Tell me Colonel, when did you first encounter Spring Heeled Jack here?
TR: Ah! That would have been in the Summer of 1877. I was in England on brief sabbatical from Harvard University. As you may know, I was a sickly lad and much of my young adulthood I spent conditioning my body to overcome my infirmities. A fit body is essential to maintain a fit mind. I spent time at endeavors such as boxing and rowing. And with my innate love of academia and the world of nature, it was inevitable that I combine the mental and physical disciplines. So it was with great excitement that I visited Aldershot Barracks in Hampshire, England, to take part in my first exhibition match.
EPD: Exhibition match? You traveled to England for boxings?
SHJ: Elephant boxing, mate.
EPD: Elephant boxing.
TR: Nothing like it in the world! Gets the blood flowing.
EPD: You is kidding.
SHJ: No, mate. They takes this pachyderm, see, and sticks gloves on both its tusks, and one on its trunk.
TR: Nothing like it in the world! The 77th Royal Fusiliers received this great beast from some Rajah that had been impressed with the troops' proclivity to wrestle the local wildlife when the unit was stationed in the British Raj. So they bundled it off back to England, where they could invite special guests to try their hand at boxing Edward.
EPD: Edward the Elephant.
TR: Yes! They became known as the 77th Light Pachyderm Scrappers. Magnificent!
SHJ: Poor blighter couldn't breath, wot with that glove on his trunk. Always making these *wharnk* sounds. *Wharnk! Wharnk!* Bloody awful.

EPD: So Colonel, you were at Aldershot to box an elephants. That's… curious.
TR: To interact with nature. Man versus beast! A true test that pits the ripe fruits of God's divine spark against the Great Brute.
SHJ: Its barbaric is what it is.
TR: Its bully!
EPD: But what brought you to Aldershot, Jack? Was it coincidences that you was both at the same place at the same time?
SHJ: Elephant boxing. What else?
EPD: But…
SHJ: Not many times a bloke gets the chance to go toe to toe with a elephant, mate. Yeah an' I missed me chance, thanks to Bull Moose over there.
TR: Bully! Nothing can stop a bull moose!
SHJ: I'll bully you in a minute, I will.
TR: Not with those flimsy stick-arms, you ragamuffin.
EPD: Both of you needs to sit down.
SHJ: No, mate! He cost me the chance to box me a elephant.
TR: Ner-do-wells such as you should never have the honor to square off against such a majestic animal.
SHJ: Well you sure fixed that, didn't you!
EPD: Is you two going to sit down or is I going to have to get the Big Stick? Now, that's better. Okay Jack, how did the Colonel cost you your chance to, and I'm not sure how many times one gets to says this, fight the elephant?
SHJ: Ted here killed ol' Eddie! Snuffed him right out, he did.
TR: Man versus beast! Besides, I did *not* kill him.
SHJ: You took a boxing glove off his tusk and stuffed it in his yapper! With one glove on his trunk and one down his gullet the poor thing couldn't get no air. Passed right out.
TR: Yes, but as soon as the ten-count was over and I manfully claimed my victory, I assure you that I cleared his airway with much vigor.
SHJ: A lot of good that did. Elephant Ed was nearly brain dead by that point. Even after they could get him all stood up, all he could do was blink. For years afterwards the 77th Light Pachyderm Scrappers had a elephant that could naught but eat, drool a little, and shite.

TR: Victory!
EPD: So, how did the troops take it? Your invaliding their pachyderm, I means.
TR: Oh, they were overjoyed. Edward had put no less than fourteen men in the hospital, and two in the grave. Yes, they were quite pleased to see a man take him down a notch or two.
SHJ: An' there I was all ready to box something, an' nothing to box but a retarded elephant! Where's the challenge in that? I might as well just go push a baby down some stairs.
EPD: So you took out your rages on Colonel Roosevelt.
SHJ: What? Hell no. Bloke had just killed an elephant with his own bare hands.
TR: I did *not* kill him.
EPD: You didn't fight?
SHJ: No, but I sure gave I'm a dirty look an' a right an' proper blessing out. An I used me fiery breath to ignite his cardigan.
TR: His language was positively atrocious, and that sweater was a gift from my dear mother.
EPD: So... that's it?
SHJ: Pretty much, yeah.
TR: Why? What have you heard?
EPD: I was under the impressions that you two had fought a battles of epic proportions. Is this not the cases?
TR: Oh. That. That was quite some time later.
SHJ: Right! That was a real knock-you-on-your knickers row, yeah?
EPD: How about we discusses that, then?
TR: One of the greatest political guerilla wars of all time.
EPD: Political.
SHJ: Yeah, mate. Now that's some dirty fighting there.
EPD: Dare I ask for the detailings?
SHJ: Well its pretty simple, ain't it? I left England in 1905, went to the south Pacific for a bit, made me a fortune in coal an' copra, yeah? Then I comes to the United States, yeah? Then I throw all me money behind Taft in 1912. You know what can stop a bull moose?
TR: Nothing!
SHJ: Money, mate. Money an' yellow journalism. Taft won an' put the

nail in ol' Ted's political coffin. An' I got me a nice cushy job as Post Master General, see? So win-win, yeah?

TR: The country was sold! The people were sold!

SHJ: Sell *this*, mate!

TR: You scoundrel!

EPD: That's it? Politicings? You know… This is just not going to works.

SHJ: Eh?

EPD: I sits here listening to you two talks, and talks, and talks, and the only thing to show for it is a tale of animal abusings and political corruptions. Excuse me while I says a short prayer that I may not kill again…

SHJ: But that's wot there is, yeah? Can't re-write history, yeah?

TR: I hate to agree with this scofflaw, but he is entirely correct. That's the gist of the whole tale. Anything else would be disingenuous. And like my father always said—By jiminy, Mr. Diablo! That's a nice looking stick you've got there. What is that? Hickory? Why, I remember the time when Seth Bullock and I—

And here the interview ends. It is fair to be saying that all of us departed with different disappointments that day. For me, I had no "Fight of the Epoch" to give reportings of. No "Battle Royale." And who really were the antagonists here after all? Them versus me? Colonel Roosevelt versus the elephant? Good taste versus sensationalisms and rubbishes? Who knows? And more importantlys, does anyone really care? As so often happens, the truths does not live up to legends. But then, I supposes that is why we needs legends. However, next time I think I shall leave the delving for truths in such matters to professionals like Tomás de Torquemada and Walter Cronkite.

And that's the way it is.

Matt Guenette & Michael Theune

DRAGONFRUIT VS. DRAGONFRUIT: THE VERSUS & THE VERDICT

THE VERSUS

I. Antioxidant Dragonfruit H2O
   after Snapple

Awaken
Smelling salts? Cold showers? Shouldn't there b
a pleasant way 2 gently shake off ur
daydreams & awaken your senses?

    Mayb
a gr8-tasting H20 w/ natural
stimulants like guarana, ginseng &
caffeine?

     If it tasted like a lightly-
sweet Dragonfruit & was full of good things
like antioxidant vitamins A & E + B
vitamins & electrolytes, would u
b dreaming?
     Would u wake up only 2 b
disappointed no such H2O existed?

Pinch urself, it's already in ur hand.

II. dragonfruit

after vitaminH2O

power-C
legally, we r prohibited from
making exaggerated claims about
the potency of the nutrients in
this bottle.

                therefore, legally
we wouldn't tell u that after drinking
this, eugene in kansas started using
horseshoes as a thighmaster
or that this drink gave agnes from delaware
enough strength 2 bench press
llamas.

                heck, we can't even
tell u this drink gives u the power 2
do a thousand pinkie push-ups…just ask
mike in queens.

                legally, we can't say stuff
like that—cause that would b wrong,
u know?

vitamins + water = all you need

THE VERDICT

I. Harold Bloom

The fruit of the genus *Hylocereus*, the fleshy and fibrous dragonfruit, its red skin warm as the morning star, emerges from large, white, fragrant cactus flowers which blossom only at night, *Moonflowers, Queens of the Night*. As such, the dragonfruit participates in an archetypal Romantic dialectic in which dreaming is true wakefulness, and to be awake is to sleepwalk. Having been awed and vivified by reading *Kubla Khan*, mustn't we say that the visitor from Porlock, by bringing business to the poet and an end to the poem, does not so much awaken as much as ring a death knell for the spirit soaring on the Wings of Poesy? And yet, such chiming is key—the spirit is better revealed in such dark relief. "Dragonfruit (1)" embodies this dialectic—it is the fruit of the juice of the fruit of this Idea. How to truly *Awaken*? By an electr(olyt)ic shock so strong that, if one survived it, could, in retrospect, have only been a dream. And so one does not want to wake, away from that source, that sensation. But—and this is the true Gospel, the undeniable good news—upon waking, we still possess, even, or especially, in its absence, the extract of that dream, and we are allowed to experience it again and again. It is the miracle of the Imagination, which Keats likened unto Adam's dream: we awaken to find it truth. Text, poem, bottle of delicious juice—*see here it is—I hold it towards you.*

II. Camille Paglia

Like all great poems, "Dragonfruit (2)" finds a way to say the unsayable. Seemingly trapped in a quandary (how to speak the beautiful utterances we are not permitted to speak?), "Dragonfruit (2)" embraces, and even foregrounds, the silencing legal power structure, employing it, paradoxically, as a tool to precisely enable the (supposedly) prohibited pronouncements. Confirming power, the poem subverts it. This is a jester's routine: *Yes, master, I know I cannot say Fellatio. Yes, mistress, I know I cannot say Whirlpool.* And, indeed, such rhetorical somersaults hide, while revealing, a queer, carnivalesque world, a topsy-turvy zone of the free-play of the signifier, an imperialist, Manifest Destiny America (the West Coast of which is both inscribed and erased by the name Eugene) populated by a sideshow citizenry: a woman "bench press[ing]" "llamas," men behaving like "[Q]ueens." Just beneath the veneer of the law seethe the vitalistic impulses, erotic, animalistic, and, in the ultimate denial of the Corporation, useless. (Of what use is a pinkie push-up? A more buff affectation for tea-time? No, the point of the pinkie is that it does not point, that it makes no point.) William Blake says *Prisons are built with the stones of Law*. The poet of "Dragonfruit (2)" constructed such a prison, but only to, like God sending in Christ or the Kool-Aid Man, rend it asunder.

III. David Sedaris

Um, like, on second thought, I'll have an iced tea…

Danielle Girard Kraus

Amy vs. Herself

The tile was slick under the balls of Amy's feet, the shower filled with the musty scent of unwashed towels. The feel and smell of home after a business trip normally brought comfort; the tepid water did not. In the days she traveled, he hadn't worked on the boiler. The pipes behind the wall still rattled as though huddling for warmth. They shivered, metal clanking to metal.

It was the dishwasher the first time, just weeks before their fifth anniversary. Water spots. For weeks, the spots had gotten worse. Gently, she'd asked then urged—it was early in their marriage after all. Weeks, he'd murmured he'd get to it.

After he'd disappeared into his office, she'd run the dishwasher, listening to the metallic kicks not unlike the kicking in her own womb. Swollen and beleaguered, she'd waited until the washer had run its course, then, while the dishes were still wet—it only made matters worse if they dried— she'd taken them out and wiped the glasses by hand. The old-fashioned one he drank bourbon and soda from. The one she'd held when she thought to call a friend…She couldn't remember which one now. Surely they weren't friends anymore.

She had pressed the call button and tucked the phone to her ear, perching on a stool to rest her bloated feet, just in time to hear her husband utter her name. "Amy? Absolutely not. Amy can't know," he'd said that night.

She'd barely heard the female response when the phone and the glass fell to the tiled floor, broken glass and batteries skittering across the floor.

Cascade commercials still made her dizzy. Water stains made her furious. She'd broken some glasses that way. Not just a few. In truth, she'd gone through most of their first set of stemware, although she always told Ben and the kids it was just her being clumsy. She suspected they knew the truth.

Using the dry, rough ball of one foot, she scrubbed at the shower tiles. She'd been meaning to get a pedicure, but what use would smooth feet have been on the dirty shower floor? When the surface no longer felt slick, she adjusted the shower to its hottest setting. For a moment—between the shivers in the pipes—she could pretend nothing was wrong. Things went wrong in an old house. It had been fourteen years since the dishwasher, a fact the therapist liked to repeat as though there was a statute of limitations that had passed.

Well, fourteen years aside from those couple "slight infractions" she knew about. And five years since those. Well, five since the one and three since the other. The therapist had some way of dismissing those, too, but she couldn't remember what it was now. He would surely dismiss the boiler as he had the overflowing washing machine and the cracked engine block and the dead motherboard. That one surely meant something.

Her forehead pressed to the cool tile of the wall, she closed her eyes. There was something wrong with her marriage. There was always something wrong with her marriage. With every marriage, she supposed, though it wasn't something friends talked about. Not her friends, what few were left. Not with her. The noise of the water paused like a car's engine just before the gears engage and icy water struck her back. She screamed, loud enough for the whole house to hear, and a moment later, it was warm again.

"I'm *in* here!" she shouted, too late.

"Sorry, Mom," her son called. "I forgot."

"It's okay," she said to herself. A few minutes and someone else would do it again. In this old house, the shower was no place to lounge. She stood up straight and pumped yellow shampoo from the bottle, rubbed it into her hair, the smell of coconut and gardenia perfuming the musty air. Working efficiently, she scrubbed her scalp, pressing her fingertips into the places that held stress. So much stress, the therapist always said. And that one massage therapist, too. Tension behind her ears and at her temples, along the division of cerebral hemispheres. Men had fewer synapses left to right, the masseuse had told her, as though he could feel her plethora with his fingertips.

When she opened her eyes again, shampoo washed into one eye. She tried to open it, but it folded closed of its own accord. As it did, she caught sight of something strange on the wall. The eye was stubborn and she rubbed harder, propelled by panic that she wouldn't be able to focus, to confirm the sighting. Squinting, she searched the white tile. For a moment, she decided she'd dreamt it. But then, there it was. A fine strand of hair. She leaned down and worked it off the wall. It stuck, plastered there as though that other she—whoever she was—had left it to mark her territory.

A long hair. Shoulder-length, Amy guessed, but perhaps even longer. She used her fingers to slide it up the tile and into the grout where she could finally free it from the wall. She held it up. Eight inches at least. With her free hand, she fingered her own head of hair, the damp curls four or five inches at the longest parts. To be absolutely certain, she pulled one free.

It was tough to get hold of just one wet strand, so she ended up with a dozen of her own, torn out between her fingers. She pressed them to the wall and carefully fanned them out, stretching the curls straight with the pads of her wet, pruning fingers. The skin around her chewed nails was bright red, furious, as though the effort was too much. Finally, her own hairs were slicked straight. With the other hair laid it beside them, she felt a strange satisfaction as the tail of it crossed the grout, stretching past the others, down into the tile below.

It was three or four inches longer at least. Her hair hadn't been that long since before the kids were in school, a decade at least. She stared at the evidence, studied it while she soaped her body and rinsed. It was more or less the same color as hers; it even had some curl, though not corkscrews like hers. She shut the shower off and stood listening to the slowing drip from her skin, from the spigot. The rattling pipes were finally speechless.

She stepped out and pulled a towel off the rack, put it to her nose. The towel smelled dank like the shower had, like it did now again, after the brief bloom of shampoo had faded. Had she been expecting another scent?

She looked at the terry cloth loops, the faded butter color now tinged with the blue of some darker wash. The long-haired woman might have used that towel. She glanced across the two towel bars, each of their four towels accounted for. Surely, that woman had used one of them. She wrapped the cloth across her shoulders, lifted it to dry her locks, ran it down her back and wiped it swiftly around each leg. She went to take it to the rack, to hang it up and instead let it fall to the floor. Her robe hung on her hook, the same pink flannel robe with roses that she'd worn at the hospital when her children were born. She slid it off the hook and into the trash. So much would change now. All of it could change.

Inside terror slithered its tentacles around her belly. She stood naked in her closet and stared at the rows of their clothes—dark suits on both sides, his dress shirts, her blouses. What did one wear to end a marriage? She walked her fingers along the hangers on her husband's dress shirts. What had he worn?

Surely, it didn't matter, she told herself, but she felt frozen there as though the toughest part of confronting him was hinged on the right outfit. Finally, she decided on jeans, a turtleneck sweater. Green. It was always a good color on her. Not too cool, not too warm. She had a red one, too, but that seemed too much.

She dressed quickly and brushed her hair, imagining she was brushing the other woman's hair, the mane. The brush struck her shoulder, catching a bristle in her sweater. She worked awkwardly to get it unsnarled, pulled a loop of yarn loose in the knit and smoothed it back down until it was almost unnoticeable.

She set the brush on the vanity and turned to the door, ready. As she passed through the bathroom, she heard voices from the kitchen. His nasal laugh and then another one, lighter, feminine, flirty. A voice as familiar as her own. She crept down to the landing to see that beautiful face. The nose dainty, unlike her own flat, wide one, bright blue eyes to her somber hazel. Long hair in a loose wave that swung across her back when she talked. Narrow hips and long, athletic legs, things she'd never have now that forty had come and gone.

She ducked into the laundry room to forward the wash that had gone undone. Loaded the dryer an armful at a time then shut the door and pressed the button. The dryer would not start. She checked the door—

shut firmly; the plug—in completely; the lights—still working. Changed the setting and heard the churning of plastic and metal, smelled burnt hair. She yanked the door open and hurried from the room. She had meant to escape back upstairs but the wood floor in the hall creaked beneath her, water damage from ten or twelve years earlier. The sound gave her away and from the kitchen, they both looked up.

No words rose in Amy's throat as she forced herself into the room, searching for a reasonable purpose, for an excuse to come and go quickly, the desire for confrontation gone.

"The dryer won't start," she said though much of the volume was lost through tight lips.

Ben didn't look up. "Yeah," he said. "The kids' shower's backed-up, too."

As the floor creaked with her every breath, Amy felt the shivering pipes and the water marks and the overflowing washer and the engine block and the dead motherboard and the breathless dryer, and it was too late to stop so she lifted her car keys from the thick stack of bills and catalogs and junk mail he'd left piling on the shelf.

"You going out?" he asked and she turned, wondering if she'd see pleasure on his face. Or relief. But he wasn't looking at her at all.

She didn't answer but opened the door to the garage and stepped out. Without a purse, without shoes, without a jacket. A last glance back and she felt pain where the terror had been before. Terror had tentacles but regret had something sharper. Regret had teeth like a shark, rows and rows of them. When one was lost, it grew a replacement, stronger and sharper.

The doorknob was in her fingers when she heard the words the other woman uttered, light with the innocence of youth. "What's wrong with Mom?"

She did not wait for the answer.

KYLE MINOR VS. ELSE RICHTER

Written By: Kyle Minor
Art By: Joshua D. Archer

MY SLEEP WAS LIKE A LONG SWIM...
...AND THE WATER THE VOICE OF ELSE RICHTER.

Kyle Minor vs. Else Richter

BACK STRAIGHT!
I KNOW YOU...
I'VE KNOWN YOU ALL MY LIFE...
YOU ARE EVERY STUPID BOY I'VE EVER MET...

Kyle Minor vs. Else Richter

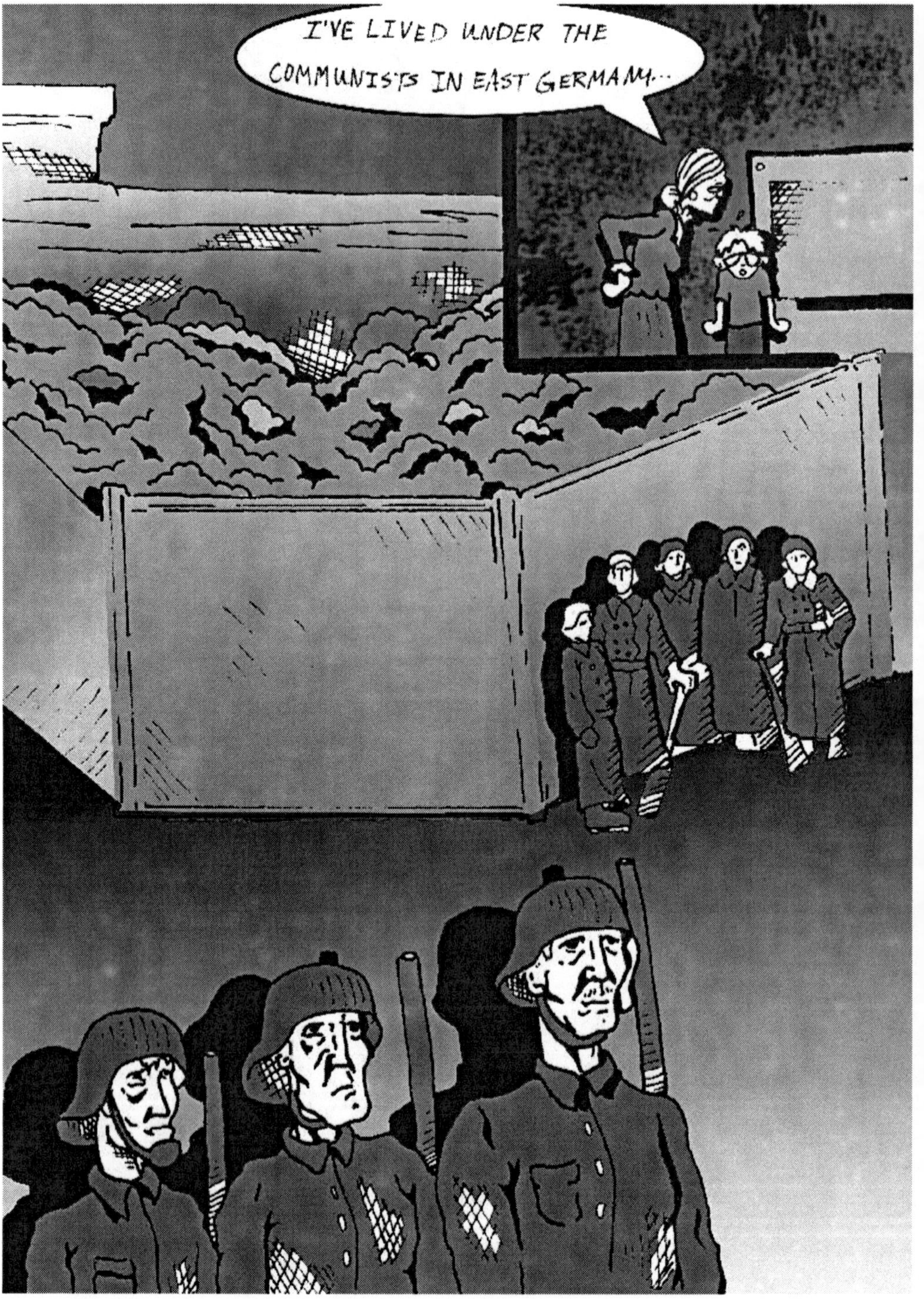
I'VE LIVED UNDER THE COMMUNISTS IN EAST GERMANY...

AND I'VE LIVED UNDER THE GODLESS WEST...
GIRLS GIRLS GIRLS GIRLS
XXX DOLLAR DRAFTS XXX
GIRLS GIRLS GIRLS GIRLS

AND I'M PROUD TO BE AN AMERICAN, BUT NOT WHEN I SEE YOUR MESSY DESK YOUR CRAYONS AND PENCILS AND ERASERS...
I SAY IN DISARRAY!

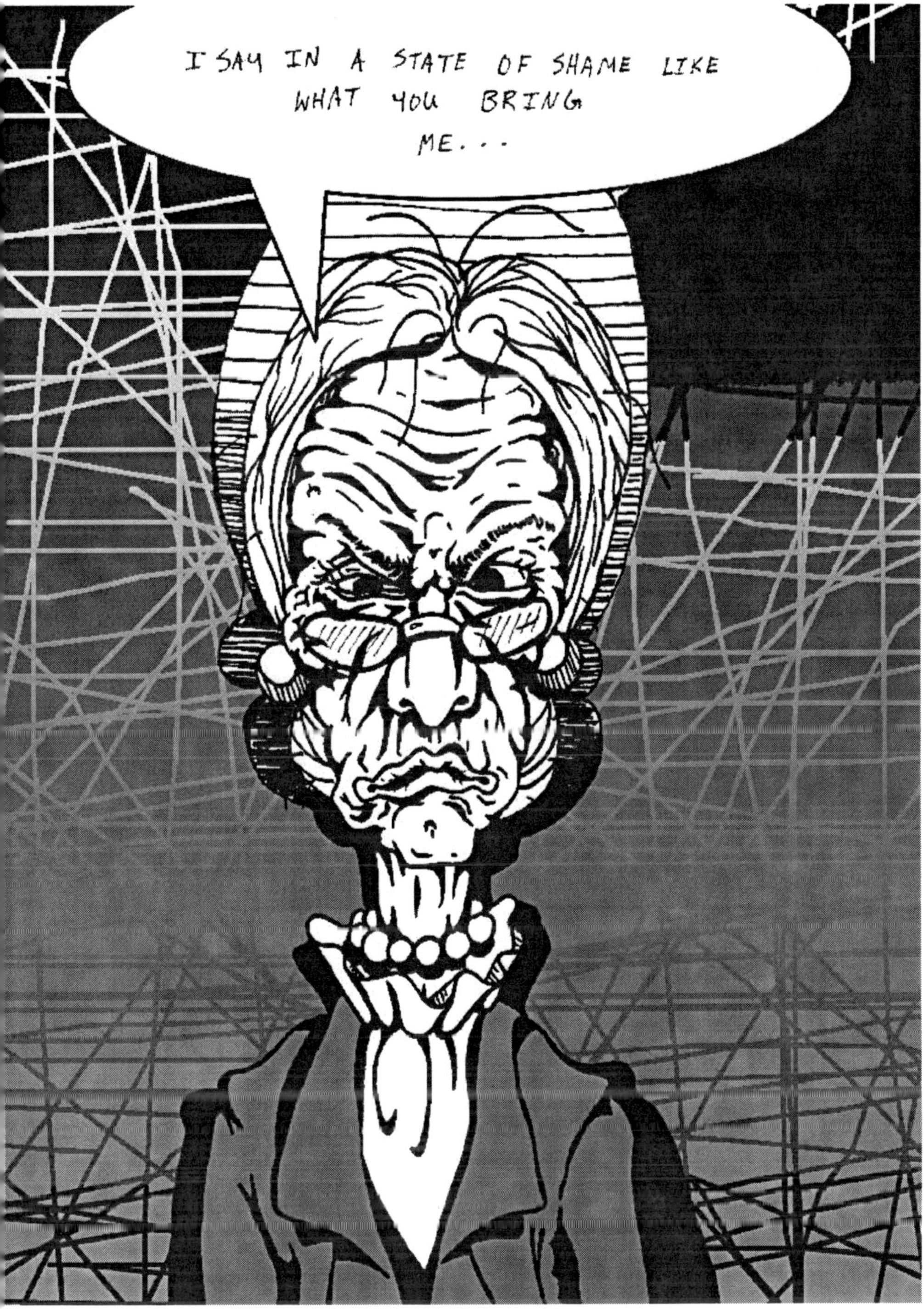
I SAY IN A STATE OF SHAME LIKE WHAT YOU BRING ME...

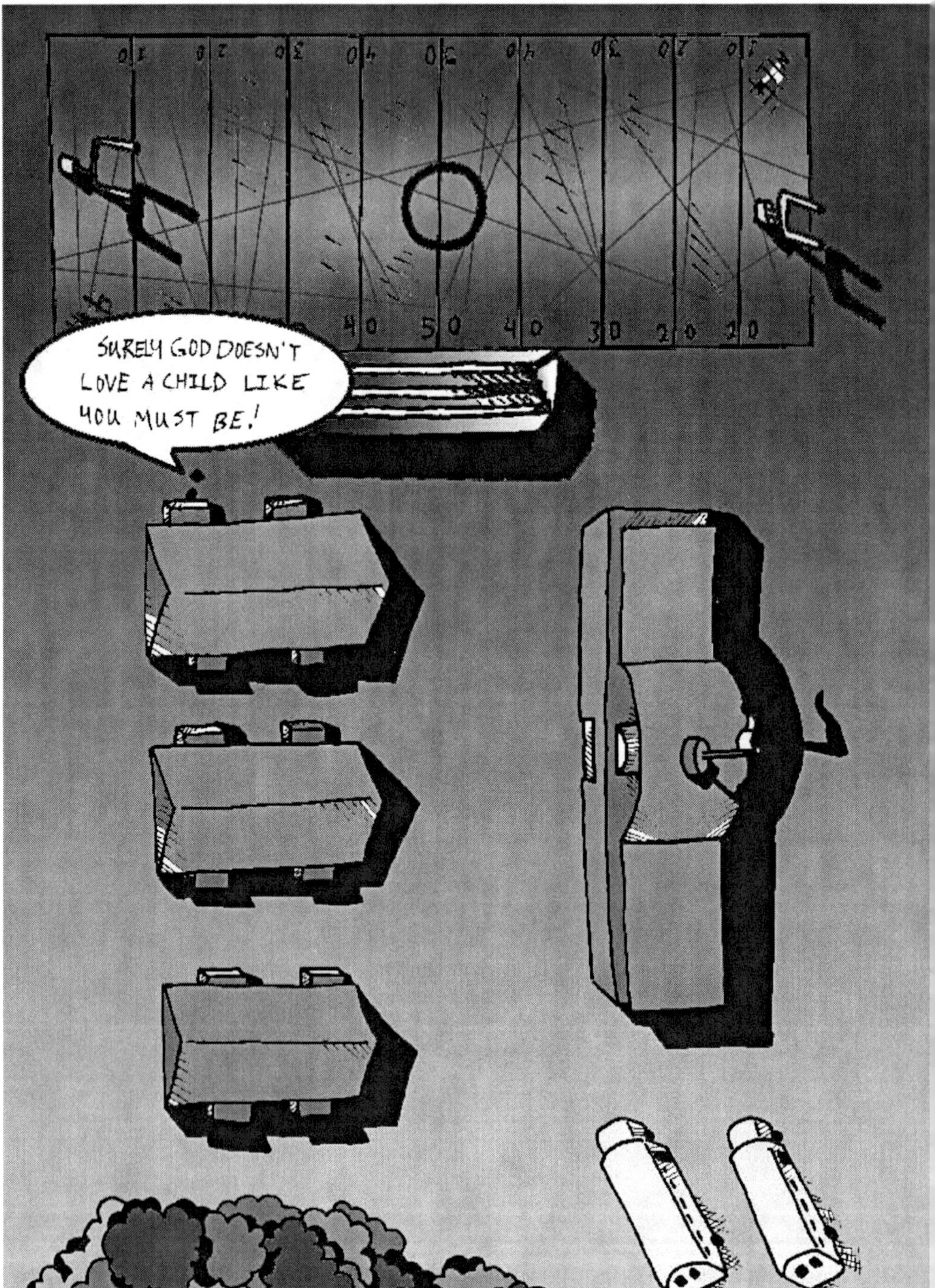
SURELY GOD DOESN'T LOVE A CHILD LIKE YOU MUST BE!

IT WAS THEN I KNEW SHE HAD FLED THE IRON CURTAIN, THE GUARDS WITH THEIR GUNS...
BRAVED THE RIVER AS THEY SAID, CARRYING HER ELDERLY FATHER, HER MOTHER, HER AUNT...

THREE SWIMS BACK AND FORTH DOWN THE SPREE RIVER...
UNDER THREAT OF BULLET AND DROWNING AND CAPTURE...

The Student Body
vol. 13 no. 12
FIFTH GRADE

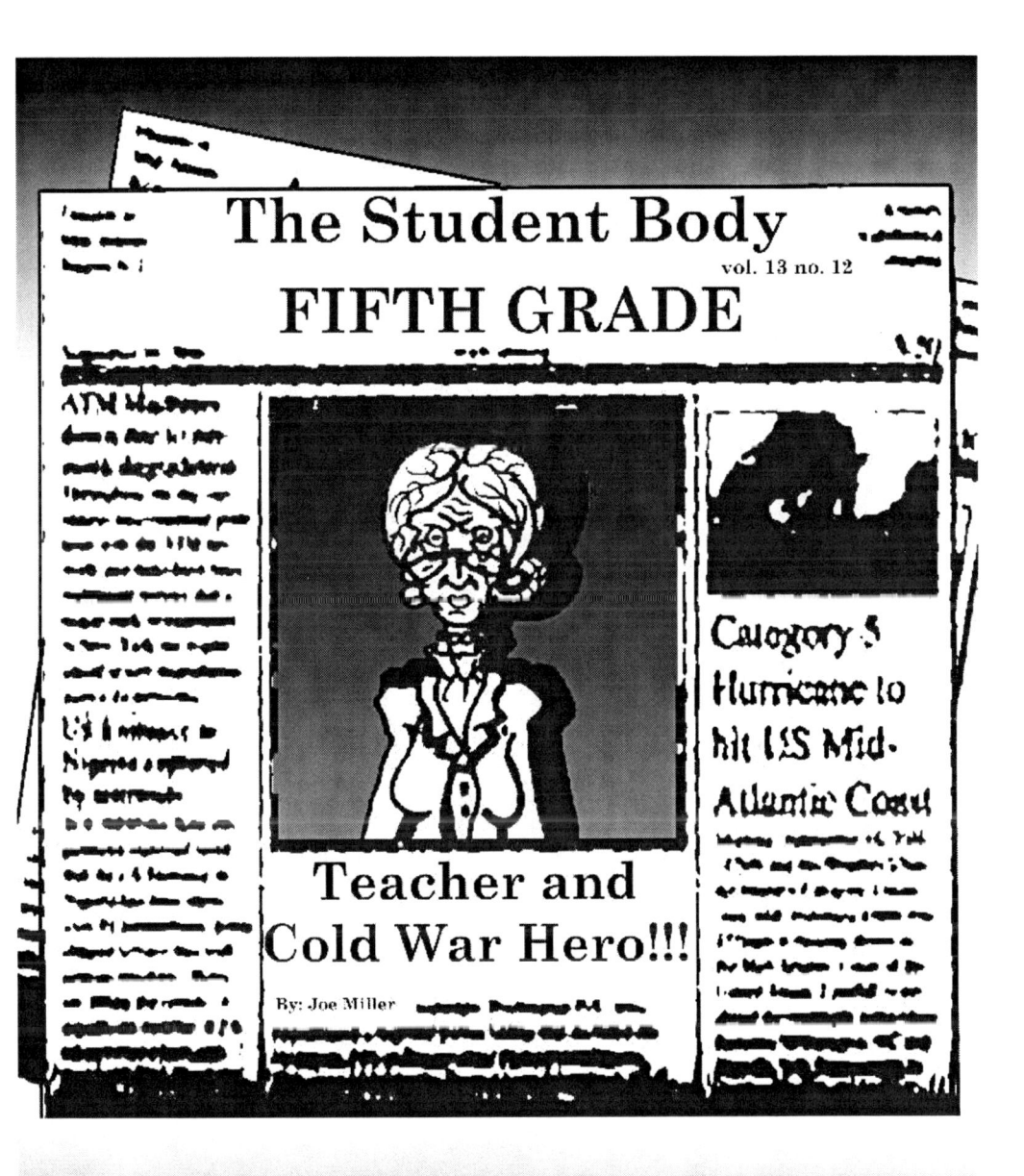

Teacher and Cold War Hero!!!

By: Joe Miller

Category 5 Hurricane to hit US Mid-Atlantic Coast

SO SHE COULD MAKE HER WAY TO WEST PALM BEACH, FLORIDA...

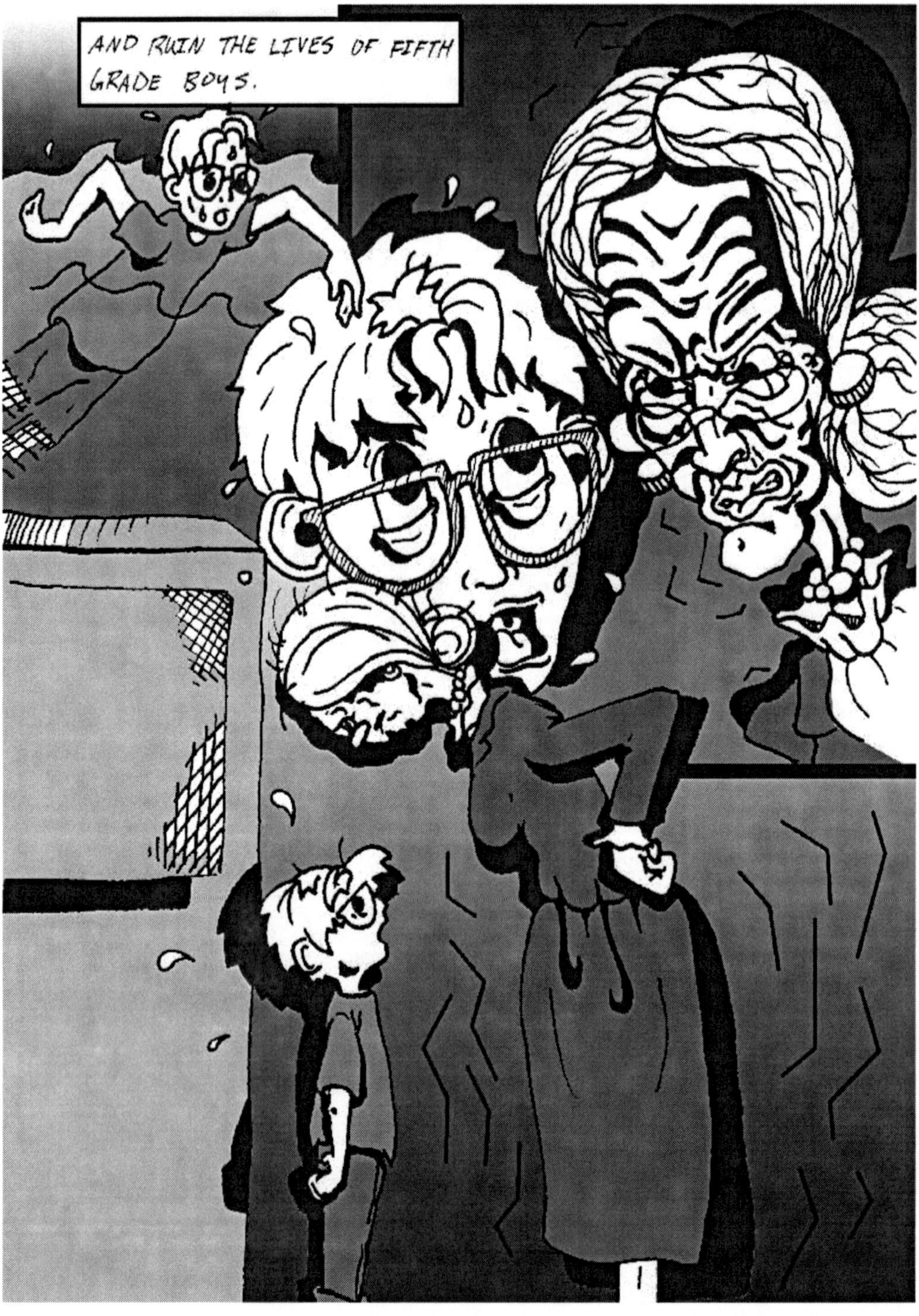
AND RUIN THE LIVES OF FIFTH GRADE BOYS.

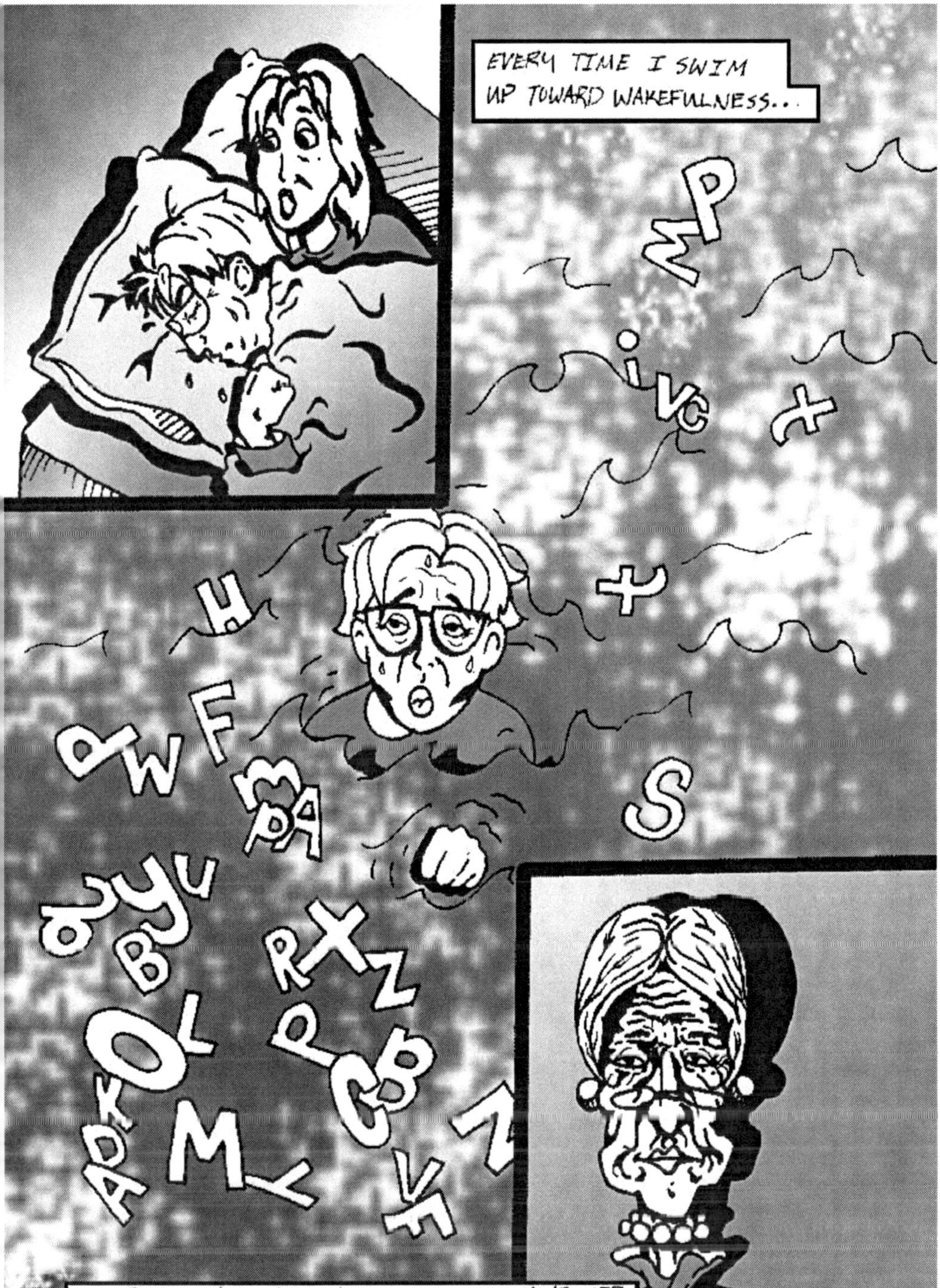
EVERY TIME I SWIM UP TOWARD WAKEFULNESS...
... EVEN THOUGH SHE'S DEAD NOW, I HEAR HER.

Susan Woodring

AMELIA EARHART VS. THE 'BURBS

What happens when you run out of gas while hopping across the Pacific Ocean in a scrappy twin-engine cloud buster is you fall from the sky, crash into said ocean, and float about, clinging to a bit of wreckage for the better part of a century. What happens when you run out of gas while limping from Los Angeles to Chicago in a used Buick of undeterminable age is you shudder to a stop in a bank of highway weeds, climb out, and lean against the stalled vehicle while April sunlight warms over you like it does in those shampoo commercials on television. A line of soulless cars zoom by. The year is 1978 and the world is full of incantations for glossy long hair streaming behind young, meandering girls in sunny fields of tall grass.

    What happens next is, just as you're ready to hoof it to the next available service station three or more miles down the highway, a sexy red Mustang comes to a smooth stop on the highway shoulder behind you, and Bev Harrison's hunky nineteen-year-old son with wavy blonde hair and white teeth gleaming up a Love-Boat smile steps out. He says it looks like you're having a bit of trouble on your journey, and you smile back, yes, you are experiencing a little setback. He offers you a ride, and you accept, sliding onto the white leather passenger seat while he cranks up some jiggly tune that reminds you of your carefree childhood in flat Kansas where you danced barefoot in a slip of a white dress under portraits of dead benefactors and gilded gold mirrors gracing the octagonal walls of your maternal grandmother's dance chamber. You don't yet know that the boy is Bev Harrison's son, or who Bev Harrison is, or why the nineteen-year-old knows just where to take you, but soon, all of this will fall into place. (It has to do with destiny and the command of the Ladies' Auxiliary Club and your own intense desire to tuck down into the geographical center of the nation.) The Mustang carries you to your new home, an apartment over the garage of a widow named Shirley Doffle whose house is the third split-level on the left once you and the nineteen-year-old turn onto Lorikeet Lane. This is presented to you as an optional residence—it has already been determined you will teach math and science at the local middle school. A moment of thought, a willingness to abandon the wrecked Buick (not to mention the soggy Lockheed L-10E), and you accept.

A few words about your new neighborhood, called the Hills. It sits in the center of suburbia, located exactly between Chicago and farmland. If you stand on the back deck of a house on Cockatoo Place and look northward, through the industrial haze of early twilight, you can just make out the jagged skyline of that great Midwestern city. If you move across Lorikeet Lane and Harlequin Avenue, you can, from the vantage point of another, nearly identical back deck, look over miles of corn, soybean, and wheat, planted in agonizingly straight lines across a great ocean of sameness.

The husbands mostly work in the city; the women—those who work outside their homes—are employed at the local shops, schools, and libraries. The Vietnam War and that distant Summer of Love have worn the housewives out, and they ignore the evening news, which their husbands nightly doze over in their easy chairs. The women have caught the wig-craze and keep styrofoam heads with different versions of themselves on their dressers or on the top shelves in their closets. They believe in Women's Liberation in moderation. To satisfy their businnessy yearnings, they sell things to each other. On your first week in the Hills, you are visited by the Avon lady, the Welcome Wagon, a teenaged girl on a paper drive, and a neighborhood lady selling a window sparkler that is her own creation, mixed up in her bathtub and sold in mason jars. You spy from behind the ruffles of gingham curtains women in green polyester dropping invitations to Tupperware and Mary Kaye parties into the mailbox mounted by your door. You attend, and the parties are terrible, these women talking up experiential learning techniques and the value of real cream applied directly to their faces. Each time, after the demonstrations, you take out your checkbook and sign over the money from those hours of explaining molecular biology to blue-eyed Suzy-Q and buff little Johnny to purchase space-age plastic tea sets and round-the-clock eye shadow. It works—these women *love* you, and you've never been the type to connect with other members of your gender. (You were strictly a daddy's girl, growing up.) Several weeks of this go by, and finally, Bev Harrison herself summons you to coffee.

The invitation is not delivered to your mailbox, but rather by the hunky nineteen-year-old whom you haven't seen since he and his erotic Mustang transported you to your place in the Hills. He is a ploy, a temptation—even you can see this is the case, but the boy is damned good-looking and your time adrift was decades long. When he touches your arm, says, Come with me, you are unable to say no.

Where are your flight patterns now? Your sea charts and navigational tools, your gauges and compasses and instinct? Your guttural yearning for lift-off, the sensation of denying that one most defining natural force—that is, your shirking off of gravity itself?

Because now, as you link arms with the nineteen-year-old, as you lean into him, him taking you down Lorikeet Lane, you waving rather helplessly to the women who come out on their front steps to watch you go, winking and smiling to each other, calling out their hellos to the boy, you have never been so thoroughly weighted. You feel every gram of your total mass, a number you might be able to name to the tenth place behind the decimal-point if you only stopped walking and paid full attention to the material reaches of your being.

You arrive at the Harrison house, and the boy deposits you in a room with a white rug and a white couch and a white-haired but otherwise surprisingly youthful-looking woman. Bev Harrison does not rise from her white leather chesterfield, but instead nods at you, gesturing for you to take a seat on a plush ottoman opposite the couch. At your elbow, on a TV tray, is a delicate teacup, white with blooming roses rising up around its sides, steaming coffee inside. There is a tiny carafe of cream, a spoon, and a miniature sugar dish with a matching rose pattern.

You're comfortable? she asks, and her voice is much lighter than you had expected, much more like tinkling wind chimes and completely unlike a wide-girthed baritone, which is what you have come to expect since the neighborhood ladies always pronounce the word *Bev* in a whisper, eyes bright with significance. She *is* a large woman, with gold bands and precious stones winking from her fingers, and her eyes are snapping green, illuminated from within.

Settling in all right?, she asks. She raises her arm to gesture and the mild scent of her *Jean Naté* dusting powder is dispersed, mixing with the dark smell of coffee that you take, finally, black.

You answer both questions in the affirmative and without further small talk, Bev Harrison comes right to the point. You, lady navigator, she intones, have been selected to participate in a talent show. You do have talent, don't you? the grande dame blinks. Here, you say nothing, but only drink the coffee, utterly bitter, as you like it, as you used to perk it on your own stove years ago, as you used to prepare it for your father when you were a girl. Your mind begins to piece together a refusal.

The show is to be a competition between your very own the Hills and the Pines, a nearby suburb whose streets are not named after tropical birds, but instead pay homage to old school movie stars—Janet Leigh Lane, Judy Holliday Street, Esther Williams Way. Judged by a local television news anchor, the prizes for individual categories include gift certificates to restaurants and pet grooming facilities, magazine subscriptions, fruit baskets, and a shopping spree at Food World, given to the Best Overall. Bev Harrison's voice turns squeaky when she admits that some husky strumpet from Joan Crawford Circle *always* takes the grand prize, the shopping spree and all its associated glory. The entire neighborhood touts the victory at every social function for the entire year, from the Christmas Party for orphans in Schaumburg to the May Pole Festival in Oak Park. It's pure embarrassment for the ladies of the Hills, an inescapable, burning humiliation.

Not this year, Bev Harrison insists. This year, we have our flyer, our very own pretty little bird. Her eyes crinkle; she is smiling. Whatever you need, we can get you, she says when you start to offer your arguments. Airplane, jumpsuit, sparklers, what-have-you, she waves her hand. All is granted. Bev Harrison pictures it this way: a sky show over the high school football stadium, the spectacle of you in a bomber jacket and aviator goggles flying loop-de-loops in the air. (It's all right if you swoop down low enough to frighten everyone; it's all right if you graze the face of the high school annex building.) You cannot say no, only rise up to try to convince the great lady, who, smiling that way, the perfect evil grin, is increasingly surrounded by an unearthly milky glow—white smoke—that you are unable to make the kind of show she is hoping for. I have my limitations, you tell her. You must practice, she says.

Adonis-boy is called to escort you home, and as you go, the neighborhood women again standing by the way to watch, you whisper to him that you can't do this, that you *won't* fly. Your final aeronautical disaster was just that—final. But the boy doesn't listen, he holds your arm to his side with such power it hurts and he hisses through his clamped toothpaste smile, You *will* fly. Don't you believe it?, he asks. His crippling grip on your arm and his menacing tone scares the hell out of you, but you are having trouble focusing on your fear, or even on the pain. As you pass the houses on Lorikeet Lane, you imagine each one dropping suddenly into the earth, housewife included, and you can see the green spring lawns settle over their disappearing rooftops like an ocean taking a sunken ship.

Days pass. One afternoon, a 1977 Cessna 404, the red-nosed, red-winged *Titan,* is delivered to Shirley Doffle's backyard, and you scramble to discover a new talent, reasoning that though you won't fly, perhaps Bev Harrison will be satisfied if you accomplish some other great feat. A worried little mouse of a piano teacher on Cockatoo counts out Mozart on her metronome, instructing you on which notes to play, but you have no sense of pleasing melody. You match the notes on the page with the piano keys, but it doesn't lift off; it doesn't become music. Though you remember fondly your days of dancing as a child, you find your lack of internal rhythm further handicaps you when you set out to learn tap. The high school drama teacher from California is young and headstrong—she doesn't shrink from matching forces with Bev Harrison—but you cannot muster a believable degree of melancholy for a Hamlet soliloquy, nor can you master the precise comedic timing of an amusing Phyllis Diller number. In your first week of trying, it is further discovered you can't juggle, sing, mime, or read Tarot cards, even if you fake it.

And then, while attending to household chores, you are saved. A little-remembered skill from childhood returns to you one evening as you stand washing dishes. Your hands occupied, there is nothing to do but remember shooting rats in the woods with your father's hunting rifle. You couldn't sew or assemble pies, nor flirt convincingly, not at any age, but you could hunt. Your father, a lawyer with an ever-floundering career, was happy to shrug off an afternoon of work and school you in wilderness-living. You were rapt. You were a great markswoman, felling rodents by the dozens.

No rats, he told you one afternoon, no guns. He produced a bow and arrow from a plain brown shopping bag, and as these new weapons were displayed, the pleasure in acting ancient hunter was instantly lost. You were only ten and now you could see, in the way your father's face fixed itself in serious attention as he examined the instruments, as he pulled back on the bow, affixed the arrow, and immediately failed, the arrow snagging, jumping out and falling flat like a sprung paperclip, that the games of children had taken the place of the proper advancement of adult pursuits. What now? Your father had left his office-job for an afternoon of weapon-shopping and was now frustrated with the bow-and-arrow pieces (had he gotten them at a *toy* store?) that would not work right in his clumsy hands.

For the first time, your father appeared as silly to you as he did to your grandfather, your mother's father, a rich man with little patience for failure. Reproachfully, you picked up the bow and arrow set, marched off a short distance, reared back, and shot. It hit a tree trunk, not the intended target, but it was still far better than he had done, and it began in you the desire that was usually found in sons—you *would* eclipse your father. Teeth gritting, dress torn, it was wonderful and terrible to have such an amazing job to accomplish. And you did, again and again, marching out to target practice, or, with great show, tagging a single tail feather from a blue jay. (So much better, years later, was the *flying*! Your father, in his fifty-odd years, could barely operate an automobile.)

Singing is not for you, and neither are the dramatic arts; what is left is the primitive art of bow and arrow. You find, on a quick perusal of the city, a number of outdoors shops with ample archery equipment and set yourself up below the widow's back deck to practice flinging arrows into the sky. You are determined and naturally skilled and it isn't long before any bird—any crow or pigeon to come from the city, any black bird, sparrow, or cardinal to flutter in from the high cornfields—*any* bird who dares pass over Shirley Doffle's property drops dead from the sky.

You are certain as you practice that you are being watched, by the neighborhood ladies, by the hunky nineteen-year-old turned bruiser, maybe even by the imperial dowager herself, but you are armed—*and* skilled—and so, who cares? In the mornings, you drink coffee that's so strong, it's nearly viscous, and by day, you educate young minds, more efficiently that ever before because now, in the shadow of that memory, you have no mercy, no allowances for slothfulness or folly. In the evenings, you practice, and though there is the nagging thought that you actually miss the call of the chirping Avon lady, and are surprised to find some disappointment when the polyester-clad wig-wearer skips over your box at the next round of everyday plastic ware parties. That you miss being included, though, is not motivation enough to change your plans, and you persist in perfecting your draw, your aim, your execution.

By the end of May, you are prepared. School lets out, and you sit at the back window in your little apartment over the garage, planning. Out back, Shirley Doffle takes a number of timid steps across the back yard in her flounced skirt and western-style fringed button-down. She stands beneath the nose of the plane, arms akimbo, gazing up at it. She is dressed to practice her standard talent show performance, keeping on a slow-moving mechanical bull for the duration of all four verses of "America the Beautiful." She reaches up, and her outstretched fingertip touches the tip of the plane. In the observance of that one small motion, the rest of your plan neatly unfolds itself.

It goes on without the anticipated hitches. Shirley Doffle, a tough old lady, is a committed student and she learns the controls and rituals, the distance-judging and the ability to read wind speeds and altitudes with little trouble. (To think, these ladies have been wasting her on mechanical bulls!) You take her out on day trips across the farmland, and night flights over the city, the old woman always at the controls, her movements precise, each one timed in perfect accord with the flashing instruments, the glowing panel. Bev Harrison, you are sure, is properly deceived. From the air, the Hills' rooftops are perfectly aligned, and you can once again feel the admiration of the neighborhood ladies, watching the tiny plane make slow progress across the sky. Bev Harrison lifts her embargo, or possibly, it is due to your taking fewer target practices; whatever the case, the Avon lady returns, and once again, invitations to teas, luncheons, and cosmetics showcases flood your mailbox. You vie to never again attend such an event—to do so would jeopardize the plan—but, the temptation is much stronger than you anticipated. You even find yourself gazing up the street, hoping to catch a streak of red Mustang. Yet the plan is set and you and Shirley spend evenings at her kitchen table, reviewing procedures and talking Kansas. Shirley lived there, too, as a child, though it was a different time. All things must change, the old lady says, sprinkling sugar into her tea. The day of the talent competition grows near.

What happens when you arrive at that momentous event on a balmy late June evening, just the tiniest sweetness of spring yet clinging to the air, and you are dressed not as an aviator—it is Shirley Doffle who is wearing the bomber jacket regalia, the impressive goggles—but in a sleek black jumpsuit, a sack of quivers at your back, is that Bev Harrison sits in the first row of seats in the high school auditorium and stares. Her eyes are more amused than angry, though, and she searches your face, to say, what is this? The good-looking nineteen-year-old is not in attendance, but everywhere else, the men—the husbands of the Hills and the Pines alike—sit in their business suits up and down the aisles, looking both afraid and bored—only for the men of idyllic suburbs such as the Hills are two such emotions possible simultaneously. (Here, in fact, it is the normal mode of masculinity.)

Backstage, the women are making their final preparations. This one applies black eyeliner, this one sprays her own backside with adherent before stepping into her leotard. Here, a juggler juggles oranges, here a woman in sequins sings her scales with the accompaniment of the timid little piano teacher. Elsewhere, lines are practiced, and full red lips are drawn into place. Whispers about what is happening in the other dressing room, the one used by their opponents, float among the talcum powder rising in the hot vanity lights. You stand back, in the shadows, waiting out each performance, gripping Shirley Doffle's sweaty palms.

Really, though, I'm not too nervous, she says. Are you?

No, you lie, because it is the most important moment, what happens next. Finally, it is your time. The entire assembly marches, hushed, through the emergency exit doors and into the purple-colored night. The football stadium fills and you and Shirley walk, still clasping hands, around back behind the scoreboard to where the Cessna sits like a giant bug, ready.

Shirley Doffle is not nervous because this is what is supposed to happen, and you, now realizing fully how very perfect the plan is, how close you are to executing what has become, truly, your one great talent, are calm and more prepared than you have ever been. Nothing clumsy will happen now, no running out of fuel, no dropping into the ocean like a loose comet, no derelict Buick on the side of the road.

This is for my father, you tell Shirley Doffle as the plane lifts off, the stadium of faces falling away. The nose points to the trees, the telephone poles, and finally, the clouds like gray cotton batting in the dimming sky. Shirley doesn't answer—she is already preparing for her first trick, a double roll.

Shirley rights the plane, pulling hard on the controls, the both of you breathless at this, the plane turning over again and again like a trained dolphin. Oo-ray, Shirley laughs, then, You're ready?

You close your eyes, concentrate, for this is good-bye. You want to remember it, how it feels to defy gravity, small loss really because there are other forces to contend with, or rather—more to the point—to *harness*. The string of a bow held taunt, the intrinsic energy in elasticity, the arrow shot.

Yes, you're ready.

This is for my father, you tell her, and now, the old lady hears.

For your father, she shouts back over the groan of the engine.

Leaning against the gear, she veers hard toward the outcrop of trees behind the scoreboard and flies, in minutes, across the greening state of Missouri. Onto Kansas, straight away in the middle, Shirley Doffle reaches back to shake your hand. Nice knowing you, she says, opening the hatch with a jerk of her arm. You fall, equipped with a parachute and a basket of arrows on your back. Pallas Amelia, you call yourself, dropping from the sky, through the dusty clouds and into the scrubby hard prairie. You hit earth near the stone house you were raised in, just down the road. Away from oceans and red Mustangs and styrofoam heads, you disappear.

Curtis Smith

THE DARK SAINT

Contrary to popular belief, Adolph Hitler did not perish in the Fuhrerbunker. Having clawed his way from that cave's nightmare of suicide and chaos, he was captured on the rubble-strewn streets outside the Reich Chancellery by a trio of Soviet shock troops. The Fuhrer had just shaved his trademark mustache, the razor clutched in his palsied hand nicking his lip again and again, the blood dribbling onto the soft mink collar of Madga Goebbels's evening coat. Delirious from his latest injection of battling chemicals, his slippered feet shuffling through the moonscape of ash and broken brick, he approached the three men with arms outstretched, his pale lips muttering *Bruder! Bruder!* Frau Goebbels's coat opened, revealing his sparrow's chest, the hairy patch above his sad, shriveled penis. The three soldiers, gaunt and hungry and so numb to death that their secret fears now concerned not surviving the war but returning home to the dreamy stillness of peace, were so transfixed by the spectacle they didn't bother to lift their rifles. *Bruder, bruder*, the Fuhrer whimpered, his hand stroking their broad, Slavic chins before he kissed each on the lips. The three comrades would later regret their decision not to simply gun down another German for within a week, they—and everyone else privy to the identity of the man who'd been swiftly whisked back to Moscow—were executed.

From 1945 to 1952, the Fuhrer was detained in one of the Czar's former vacation villas less than thirty miles from Red Square. Only the highest ranking party members attended the ritualistic tortures of the crazed, decrepit prisoner, the review stands once occupied by the royal family now packed with barrel-chested men whose war medals glistened in the sun like so many angry stars. These onlookers roared their approval as the Hun was chased down by a gang of mace-wielding, Viking-clad dwarves and their flesh-nipping Chihuahuas. They cheered as a clan of retarded, incredibly endowed brothers from the hinterlands of Turkmenistan repeatedly beat and sodomized him. After swigging back a case of vodka, Stalin and his general staff perched themselves in the hay-lined rafters of the villa's barn and pelted the ex-dictator's naked body with BB guns until the old man fell limp, his bloodied, scarecrow form twitching unconsciously with each new wound. The pellets, individually scuffed and dipped in acid, were later removed by Hitler's personal team of doctors, the same men who took his vital signs every day and who tenderly nursed him back to health after each brutal humiliation.

On a moonless October night in 1952, Hitler suffered a stroke while dreaming of the horses that had once stamped and whinnied in his father's stable. His caretakers informed Stalin that the coma was deep and death was only a matter of time. Stalin, with less than a year to live himself, ordered Hitler's doctors and the villa's entire staff shot; then he assembled the greatest medical and mechanical minds of the USSR. Perhaps the sight of the villa courtyard's blood-stained walls provided the desired inspiration, for despite the fact that Hitler's heart had stopped before they could unpack their bags, they swiftly achieved their goal. Utilizing a series of pumps and electrical impulses, the cadaver was—in a fashion—revived, the telling brain waves quivering with each insult to the Fuhrer's flesh. To this day, the corpse survives in the Kremlin's bomb-proof basement, a gray-ash ghost entombed in an oft-updated, super-oxygenated chamber. Every so often, the elaborate, hissing gurney is wheeled out, and by using a pair of thick rubber gloves built into the chamber's glass, der Fuhrer can be subjected to slaps across the bony soles of his feet, to pins stuck beneath his meticulously clipped fingernails. In a country that adores its icons, Adolph Hitler has become the patron saint of the Unforgiving, a dark angel few wish to claim but no one can deny.

Andrew Scott

Arthur Miller Walks into a Bar, A Five Minute Screenplay: Arthur Miller VS. Joe DiMaggio

FADE IN:

INT. HEAVEN - DAY

ARTHUR MILLER walks into a corner bar decked out in deep mahogany wood. CHARLIE PARKER taps the piano on the corner stage; jazz drifts across the room. Arthur is backlit by heavenly glory until the door SWINGS SHUT.

> BARTENDER
> What'll it be, playwright?
>
> ARTHUR MILLER
> Scotch and soda.

The bartender turns to make the drink. Arthur casually looks to his left; down the bar sit several prominent figures: Freud, Joan of Arc, Einstein, and Amelia Earhart.

Arthur is TAPPED ON THE SHOULDER by another man. When he turns, he finds JOE DIMAGGIO dressed in his Yankees uniform.

> ARTHUR MILLER (CONT'D)
> You gotta be kidding me.

JOE DIMAGGIO

I'm not a kidder, Mr. Miller.

ARTHUR MILLER

I know, I know — you're all business, on and off the field.

Joe takes a seat next to Arthur. The bartender returns with the scotch and soda and, without asking, pours Joe a glass of ginger ale.

JOE DIMAGGIO

Been a long time.

ARTHUR MILLER

Indeed.

JOE DIMAGGIO

I never liked you.

ARTHUR MILLER

What of it?

JOE DIMAGGIO

You're nothing special up here. We've got Dante down the street. Now that's a writer. Who are you? A 20th century nobody.

ARTHUR MILLER

I just saw Babe Ruth walking down the street with 72 virgins.

JOE DIMAGGIO

What the Bambino wants, the Bambino gets.

ARTHUR MILLER

That means you're not even the best Yankee I've seen today.

                    JOE DIMAGGIO
          How do you want to do this?
                    ARTHUR MILLER
          Do what?
                    JOE DIMAGGIO
          You know what I want.
                    ARTHUR MILLER
          To fight me?
                    JOE DIMAGGIO
          Bingo, baby. You're a bright one.
                    ARTHUR MILLER
          In heaven.

Joe nods.

                    ARTHUR MILLER (CONT'D)
              (in disbelief)
          You want to fight me...in heaven.
          Doesn't that seem, I don't know, a
          little contrary to the idea?
                    JOE DIMAGGIO
          I've been waiting.
                    ARTHUR MILLER
          I didn't take her away from you.
                    JOE DIMAGGIO
          But you were part of the problem,
          weren't you? You and everyone else.

The door OPENS again and in walks GENGHIS KHAN and a small NERDY MAN. Genghis Khan slaps the Nerdy Man on the back and they laugh.

ARTHUR MILLER
Who the hell is that?
JOE DIMAGGIO
Genghis Khan.
ARTHUR MILLER
No, the guy with the pocket protector.
JOE DIMAGGIO
How the hell should I know?
ARTHUR MILLER
He must be somebody. Look around — everyone here is famous.
JOE DIMAGGIO
Not everyone in heaven is famous.
ARTHUR MILLER
Sure seems that way.
JOE DIMAGGIO
Why, because you're here? Writers are such egomaniacs...
ARTHUR MILLER
Ambrose Bierce said an egomaniac is "someone of low taste, more interested in himself than in me."
JOE DIMAGGIO
Who's Ambrose Bierce?
ARTHUR MILLER
He's...
JOE DIMAGGIO
All I know is, you make a mess in life and then you die.

ARTHUR MILLER

And end up here, apparently. Okay, so not everyone's famous in heaven. But this place —

JOE DIMAGGIO

This place is what you make of it.

ARTHUR MILLER

You're saying somewhere deep inside, my vision of nirvana, my utopian comeuppance, is a bar?

JOE DIMAGGIO

You could do worse.

ARTHUR MILLER

My idea of heaven, whatever it is, doesn't include you badgering me.

JOE DIMAGGIO

Stick with me, playwright. You think you know everything, but you don't. You haven't even asked the important question yet?

ARTHUR MILLER

Is there a God?

JOE DIMAGGIO

What are you, a dunce?

Arthur finishes his drink. He clinks the ice around the glass. The bartender begins to ask if he wants another, but Arthur WAVES him off.

ARTHUR MILLER

So where is she, then?

JOE DIMAGGIO

There you go. Now you're talking.

ARTHUR MILLER

Just answer the question.

JOE DIMAGGIO

She's not here.

ARTHUR MILLER

What do you mean she's not here? Einstein helped make the A-bomb and he gets in? When was there ever a place that wouldn't let her in?

JOE DIMAGGIO

Don't expect to see her soon. I haven't seen her, anyway.

ARTHUR MILLER

Because of the way she died, is that it?

JOE DIMAGGIO

Why's that?

ARTHUR MILLER

The whole "unforgiveable sin" thing.

JOE DIMAGGIO

After all the evidence, you still think she killed herself?

ARTHUR MILLER

I've come to terms with it. It's the most likely result of the life she lived.

                    JOE DIMAGGIO
                (delay)
            It didn't have to be.

They sit in silence for a beat. JOE takes a deep breath and looks away. Arthur taps his fingers on the bar. The camera pans to show some of the other patrons: JIMI HENDRIX is playing dominoes with MOTHER TERESA. Joe stands up to leave.

                JOE DIMAGGIO (CONT'D)
            You make your own heaven, Mr.
            Miller. I'm not here because I want
            to be. I'm not even "me" when I'm
            here. Get me?

                ARTHUR MILLER
            In her idea of heaven, we're not
            around. We play no part.

                JOE DIMAGGIO
            You're quicker than I thought. Took
            me a long time to realize that.

                ARTHUR MILLER
            I sure miss her freckles. You know
            the ones, her clavicle...

Joe nods.

Joe pats Arthur on the shoulder and walks away. Bird brings the number to a close and the audience erupts in applause. Sitting at the bar for several more moments, Arthur finally signals the bartender for another round.

                            FADE TO BLACK.

Michael Kimball

The Girl I Thought I Would Marry When I Was Six vs. The Woman I Did Marry When I Was Twenty-Six

Dear Kathy Granger,
    Do you remember when I used to stand on the sidewalk outside of your house and yell out your name until you came outside to play with me? I didn't know that you were just my babysitter and that my mom and dad paid you to watch me. I thought that you really liked me—and not just because I was a cute little boy. I thought that we were going to get married when I was old enough.

Dear Sara Olson,
    I didn't sign the divorce papers because I wanted to be married to you for as long as I could. I was even hoping that you wouldn't be able to divorce me at all if I didn't sign them. You didn't have to go to a judge to prove that I was unfit for marriage.
    Since we really are divorced now, I think that we should split up our memories too. I want the time that we met and the time that we went to the Grand Canyon. You can have our first date and the day we got married. You can also have the day that you left me, which I have no use for. I want when we moved in together and when we bought our house, though, and I want all of the times that we sat on the couch and watched television together. You can have the times we ate breakfast together, but I want most of the dinners. There are a lot more. Maybe we should talk about all of them.

Okla Elliott

THE IMPOSSIBLE DIVISION BY ZERO:
HULK VS. HEL, GODDESS OF THE UNDERWORLD
non-fiction

My sister Vickie sat on the burnt-orange couch in the living room, talking into the phone, as Dr. Doom's faceless, pink-and-gunmetal-gray doombots closed in on the house. There must have been dozens soldiering slowly up from the road, more rocketing in from the clouds. It was raining, and I wondered whether Dr. Doom had discovered a way to control the weather. My task would be more difficult if he could fling bolts of lightning at me. Not that I was all that scared of lightning. My skin was nearly impervious organic rock; I was the Thing. I could lift-press eighty-five tons, and the cosmic radiation that transformed me into this monstrosity, this *thing*, made it so I didn't have to fear much on Earth. Then I realized I hadn't accounted for why the other members of the Fantastic Four weren't with me, so I decided they were being held in a special cell—I looked out the window and a small copse of kudzu laden poplars became a high-tech prison—and I had to destroy the doombots and save my friends. Now that I knew my purpose, I flexed my huge, rocky arms and walked toward the door, readying myself for the battle of a lifetime. And, yes, by Jesus, it felt good, *'cause it was clobberin' time!*

"He gets to live in his fantasies," Vickie said and looked at me, making sure I knew how easy I had it, as I let the screen door slam behind me with a creaking of springs and a wood-on-wood slap. "But I have to find a way to deal with all this," I heard Vickie say through the open summer windows.

I jumped off the porch, already swatting a doombot from the air and grabbing another's head and crushing it. A concentrated pulse of energy exploded against me and I flung myself to the ground, jarring my head, but then I remembered I was nearly indestructible. So, head ringing, I stood and ran farther from the house, until I couldn't hear Vickie.

This was southeastern Kentucky, about sixty miles from the Tennessee border. Argyle, Kentucky. The roads near our house were called Dog Trot, Bethel Ridge, Poodledoo Road. I make jokes about all of it now that I'm older. "Yes. Argyle, Kentucky," I say, "No relation to the socks." Or: "Main road was Dog Trot, half of which, I'm proud to say, was paved." Stuff like that. Stuff that shrinks the real meaning of the place.

And what Vickie was talking about—and was only able to talk about because our mother was asleep, as she often was in the afternoon—was that our father had just died two months before, on May eleventh, ten days after my tenth birthday, and she would be going to college at Eastern Kentucky University in less than a month. In that time, she had to find a way for me to survive living with our mother, who had most recently been diagnosed as a schizophrenic with a history of violence that had been escalating since our father's death. (At the age of ten, I didn't understand what schizophrenia was, only that crazy people on television were said to have it.) Vickie was about to turn eighteen, and even then I knew she was overwhelmed by the impossibility of the situation and just wanted to run off to college, to the sorority she had already made plans to pledge for, to the city of Richmond, Kentucky, where there were malls and movie theatres and more than a dozen restaurants—all of which seemed fantastical to someone raised in Argyle, a forty-minute drive from the nearest grocery store. I'm still amazed she didn't. It was an option. No law compelled her to ruin this and the coming years of her life. It's a story straight out of a made-for-TV movie: *Dedicated older sister overcomes impossible odds to save brother from mentally ill mother after the death of their aged father.* The studios might throw in a love interest or two, but the basic structure is there.

But I wasn't thinking of any of that as I smashed my way across our front lawn to save Mr. Fantastic, the Human Torch, and the Invisible Woman. All that mattered was withstanding the relentless onslaught.

2.

It started with the Incredible Hulk. Sarah Sallee, the strawberry-blond daughter of Mrs. Phelps, the sixth grade teacher at Garrett Elementary, was a lofty and unattained love of mine. As the Hulk, I tore planes from the sky, smashed buildings to bits, saved Sarah from the evil clutches of Soviet evil-doers. (In 1986, all evil-doers were Soviet.) But Sarah could never marry me because of the monster I was, but while others screamed in terror as I leapt miles away from the scene of carnage, Sarah looked forlornly at my green figure shrinking in the distant sky.

Or: I was calm until Kyle Durham and his cronies came to taunt me for my cheap Velcro shoes, or whatever they'd decided was the current excuse. (Kyle was the principal's son, so he never got in trouble no matter whom he tormented.) Then—fighting (unsuccessfully of course) the monster in me—I turned into the Hulk and lifted Kyle in my green and unimaginably powerful hand and squeezed until blood leaked out of his eyes and ears, the slow crunch of bone sweet between my fingers. His friends were stunned, and I dropped Kyle's corpse to the ground and looked at the mangled, motionless lump. I screamed with horror at what I'd done. No—wait—I needed to kill the other bastards as well, then I could scream with horror at what I'd done. So I stomped the cronies underfoot, and screamed with…

At one point or another I was every Marvel comic character, but I was especially drawn to the lonely, the dangerous, the darker ones—Wolverine, Cloak (who had the added advantage of running around with the scantily clad Dagger), Silver Surfer, Thanos. I am tempted to write something like: I was having fantasies of empowerment, given my powerlessness in the face of my father's death and my mother's abuse. I'm tempted because it's as clean and easy as the comics I hated as a boy—Captain America, Superman, and the like. That was part of it, sure, but I was also a boy playing with games of imagination, a boy drawn to the darker comic figures as other young boys are drawn to heavy metal or vampire movies or wearing all black. (It's fitting, and philosophically very neat, that we become obsessed with the imagery of death just as our bodies begin to feel the first biological urges to procreate.)

It is a failure of pop psychology and talk show circuits to assume that our actions are explained by the most dramatic or traumatic aspects of our lives. It strikes me just as likely that they are explained in equal measure by the mundane and trivial influences. But those who—either in the name of toughness, or due to a lack of patience for "sob stories"—dismiss the effects of abuse are equally wrong-minded. In the years since I left my mother's house, I have played The Victim, The Toughened Survivor, the Humorous Dismisser, the Pretender That Nothing Happened. But none of these roles fit. They are popular, easy, false stances—and I am disappointed I assumed them.

3.

I've wanted simply to hate my mother, but I can't. It's not as if her life has been enviable. And my parents' match-up wasn't the most opportune. By the time my father met her, he had fought in World War II, come home a mostly useless alcoholic, ruined one marriage and family, and was now in his fifties—not the time a man generally looks to start another family. (My half-sister Carol showed up at our father's funeral and spent the whole day enumerating his failings, as if to make sure that no one thought that his death absolved him of the hell he'd put her and her mother through.) Freida, my mother, only twenty at the time, took care of her grandmother, who had suffered a stroke. My father's mother was also in poor health, so he hired Freida to help out. He dropped Flora off at Freida's grandmother's house, where Freida would watch over the two old women all day, then he'd head down the road about twenty miles to the rock quarry where he worked, which was rough labor and not much pay.

By that time in her life, the woman who would become my mother had experienced more pain and upset in her twenty years than most lifetimes contain. Her father had singled her out for physical and sexual abuse; she suffered from the early stages of what would, in her forties, finally be diagnosed as her schizophrenia; and the poverty she was born into forced her to work various farm and service jobs instead of completing high school. When she was offered the job of taking care of another old woman, she must have felt like she'd won the lottery: no more long hours in the sun; now she'd just sit around, smoke cigarettes, and make sure old Miss Elliott didn't fall on her ass, maybe occasionally bringing her a sandwich or a cup of hot coffee when she complained of being cold. And the more she looked at Miss Elliott's son, wasn't he handsome with his pitch black hair, his muscles hardened from manual labor, and his ex-soldier's composure?

4.

Like many boys in rural Kentucky, I began drinking younger than the kids in the suburbs did. At ten, it was already common practice for my cousin Sam and me to steal his father's beers and drink them in the cover of a tobacco field or in the woods behind my house. His father, Gary, was an alcoholic who drank himself to sleep by eight p.m. every evening, a fortuitous habit for Sam and me. It was one of these nights that I was trying to explain quantum mechanics to Sam. I didn't know thing-one about quantum mechanics, except that it claimed things weren't what they seemed and that only smart people understood it.

My mother had been having a particularly bad episode earlier that evening, pacing the house in her bra and a pair of sweatpants, chain-smoking her Pall Malls, and yelling about how my father had ruined her life and telling me how he'd wanted her to abort me, but she just wouldn't do it, though now she wished she had. When she got like that, I knew she was going to do something crazy. And I didn't want to be in the house when she did. I called Sam, and he told me I could come over, that we'd steal some of Gary's beer and have a good night. I thought the beer tasted nasty, but I drank it anyway.

In the middle of some lies I'd made up about quantum probabilities, Sam fell into the five-foot hole Gary had hired a man with a backhoe to dig for his shortwave radio antenna. I'd been studying Morse code to take my radio license test to be more of a part of their household, one of my favorite escapes from my mother's house. (I never took the test and still regret it today, not for any real interest in shortwave radios, but just to be able to say I am licensed in Morse code. Seems like a cool idea to me. I guess I could still do it, but Morse code seems like something you should learn when you're young, like a foreign language or the harpsichord.) I laughed at Sam for having fallen in the hole. I was as drunk as only a ten year-old can be. I thought it was the funniest thing in the world that he had fallen into this big hole without even seeing it.

"Stop laughing and give me your hand."

I reached into the hole, and Sam grabbed it. I pulled as hard as I could, but Sam was thirteen and outweighed me by thirty pounds. Then, almost as if I could read his mind, I knew he decided not to get out of the hole, but to pull me down in it. When he yanked, I didn't fight, just jumped down there with him.

It was darker in the hole, and Sam handed me a can of beer from the bag he had them in.

"I hate this stupid fucking antenna," Sam said. He cursed a lot.

"Yeah, pretty fucking stupid shit," I said. "Your dad's a real asshole."

I remembered I'd been talking about quantum stuff. "And if I were the Silver Surfer," I explained, "no bullet could puncture my skin, not even armor piercing ones, because the molecular tension in my skin, harnessing cosmic energy, would be impenetrable. And I'd fly to Africa and make food by rearranging the molecules of the earth to be…"

"Will you shut the fuck up?" Sam asked casually, as if he'd made the most reasonable request he could imagine. "I mean, you never stop fucking yapping. Just. Shut. Up."

He looked at me cold, and I shut up. I felt air swelling in my chest, pressure behind my eyes, and I knew that if I cried, Sam would just yell at me and call me a faggot or a pussy and not want to hang out with me, so I breathed out heavily and controlled myself. Sam jumped up and grabbed the edge of the hole and climbed out.

"Go home," Sam said. "I don't want to hear you talk anymore." He knew what it meant to send me home. He knew what I had there.

I didn't understand what had happened, why he'd become so mean all of the sudden. I sat in the hole and listened to his distancing feet. I didn't want to go home, but I didn't want to be around Sam. I don't remember if I went home or not, but I do remember sitting in the muddy hole for a long time, finishing all the beers Sam had left behind. I got drunker and drunker and wondered if life was purest shit.

5.

I stood on the steps in front what would be our new apartment, my new home, in one month—such a short amount of time. It had been nearly two years since our father had died. Car fumes filled the air, car engines revved, horns honked in the distance. The trees were small and decorative, none of them sturdy enough to climb. I wondered what I would do with no trees to climb. Then I thought of girls and about all those movies and television shows set in cities where teens were always having sex and doing drugs, and I thought maybe this wouldn't be so bad after all.

I was going to be allowed to live with my sister. There were discussions of foster homes because the State of Kentucky was uncomfortable with letting a twelve-year-old live with two college students. But in Kentucky, at age twelve a person gets a say in where he lives. All you have to do is bullshit some psychologists with clichés about families staying together and prove that you're adult enough to be part of the decision in how your life is going to be. My mother was unsuitable. That much everyone agreed on. All I had to do was show the cigarette burns on the insteps of my feet to prove that one. I didn't care so much about the burns as I did about getting to Richmond and living with my sister.

I heard a door upstairs shut and wondered if it was Vickie, finally ready to go. I was Daredevil—my senses heightened to superhuman levels, my radar compensating for my blindness—so I closed my eyes and listened for footsteps on the stairs, trying to determine the weight of the person. I sniffed the air, testing for my sister's perfume but instead got a faceful of city smells and the oily stench of cheap apartment parking lots. It was the keys that did it. As she walked up behind me, I heard her keys jingle just so, the way that only Vickie's keys did. I opened my eyes and turned around. Vickie was wiping her eyes and her face was splotchy, *really unattractive* I thought before I could stop myself, feeling bad, and then I saw that she was crying and felt worse. So I turned back and closed my eyes again, and when she put her hand on my shoulder and said, "Okay, let's go," I pretended I didn't see her crying.

I can't imagine doing what she did. Eighteen years old. I have students that age now who can't manage to show up on time to a two p.m. class. Imagining them adopting a twelve year-old and working full-time at McDonald's and completing a math degree…unthinkable. I could write something like: We do what we must. But so many people don't or wouldn't have. As I've mentioned, Vickie has made a cottage industry of reminding me of her sacrifices, but I never argue with her. I mean, fuck it, right? Let her feel proud. She should. I know for a fact that I'm not made of the kind of stuff that would make me capable doing what she did.

As we pulled out of the parking lot, I looked over at Vickie, and her McDonald's uniform reminded me of a costume from a comic book. "Hey, you've got your McDonald's costume on," I said. "You're like the Super-Chef or Hot-Vat or something."

Vickie laughed and the watery snot from her crying nearly shot out of her nose, which made us both laugh. "Or Dr. Deathburger," I said.

"No, no," she said. "The Bun Woman!"

That wasn't a very good one, but I laughed anyway. "Yeah, and I'm your side-kick. Get it? " I said. "You know, like, what kind of side-kick would you like with your super-hero meal?"

We laughed a little more and then we were quiet. I was going to ask Vickie if she would buy me a comic book. I had enough money for one, money she'd given me, but I wanted two. I would ask her for the comic book later, I decided. I turned on the music. I can't remember what came on the radio, but I prefer to think of it as something charmingly dark, maybe "The Boxer" by Simon and Garfunkel. As was my habit at the time, I looked for references to my and my sister's situation in every song. "The Boxer" was one my self-important favorites. It described me as a fighter, a poor boy, a person possessed of secret knowledge only hardship can imbue, and a person with an unattainable longing for a home forever lost. So, let's make it the soundtrack to this memory, even if it wasn't.

"Do you like the place?" Vickie asked as we drove toward campus, where John Raleigh, a male friend of hers would entertain me while she was at work (over the years, Vickie would get many free hours of babysitting from guys trying to prove how sensitive and understanding of my sister's difficult situation they were). And I was eager to hang out with John, because he was a physics major and would talk to me about science and math. He explained how the things in my comics could maybe make sense, and he gave me his old textbooks for me to take back with me when I went home to my mother's house.

"Yeah," I said. "I think this is going to be great."

"Just one more month," Vickie said. "That's all you have to wait."

"You're a poet and don't know it," I said, but she didn't laugh.

6.

It was the next day, back at home, that my mother came into the kitchen, and I became Doc Sampson. I was smart, strong, and I had a really cool green ponytail. I kept eating my cereal, looking at the milk made reddish by the cereal, and thought how sweet it was going to be.

"You need to be in bed," my mother said.

"I have homework to finish," I said, knowing I was one of the most talented scientists in the world, trained in psychiatry and physics and mechanics, knowing that for me the work I was doing from the algebra book Vickie had bought me would be easy. As Doc Sampson, I was one of the foremost specialists in Gamma radiated super-beings (e.g. the Hulk, She-Hulk, the Abomination, and myself). I had important equations to work out and difficult quandaries to pursue. Why would Mom want me to go to bed now?

"It's summer," Mom said. "You don't have homework."

I heard the bowl break against the wall and saw the splatter of milk before I knew what had happened. I turned and faced my enemy. It was Hel, Norse Goddess of Death, and her grotesque form—her left side that of a corpse, her right side a vicious woman—shot fear into me. I changed faster than I could keep track. I tried Quicksilver, who could run at 175 miles per hour, but Hel caught my arm. I became Spider-Man, whose reflexes made it nearly impossible to hit him, but Hel was faster. She hit me in the ear, then grabbed a cold, wet washcloth from the sink and shoved it into my face. Little particles of food went into my eyes.

A dark world of death and hatred opened up behind her, demons' faces whirling, ecstatic with immortal pain. "When a command from The Goddess of Death is heard, it will be obeyed!" she screamed, her voice the roar of a seven-headed lion.

"Spare me," I pleaded but already knew there was no use, so I became Wolverine, whose healing factor can repair any damage. But Wolverine wasn't strong enough to fight Hel. I needed the Hulk.

I felt adrenaline pumping, bringing my strength to levels beyond human comprehension. I tore a chunk of rock and earth from the ground and threw it with the force of a dozen locomotives. But Hel swatted it to the side. She was invincible so long as her victim feared her; that was her most important power. She could bring on all the force of Death and the Underworld, could channel the strength of an army of demons—but what was an army of demons to the Hulk?

I punched her in the stomach. I punched wildly, hitting her face and her breasts and her arms, her neck, flailing, eyes wet with rage. But even in my anger I was embarrassed to have touched my mother's breasts, though I kept hitting her anywhere I could. I wanted to kill her more than anything I had ever wanted in my twelve years on Earth. I wanted my mother dead. Then there was a dark jarring thud against the side of my head and I saw the kitchen floor just before I hit it and she was on my back hitting me again.

"I wish you would die," I said, feeling my lips slide on the linoleum as I did. "Fuck you. I wish you would fucking die."

It was the first time I'd cursed at my mother. My skin tingled and a scared place like falling opened up in my stomach. I knew this was going to be a bad one. I tried to predict where on my body she would put out cigarettes. Her favorite places were where no one could see, but I figured she'd be too angry to think about it and put them out on my face this time. Maybe my eyes. In what seemed like an impossible amount of time, I mourned the loss of my sight, wondered how life would be blinded. But she just stopped. She stood up from the tangle we'd made of ourselves on the floor and walked into the living room. "I can't believe you'd say such a thing," she said. "And to your only mother."

I lay on the floor for a few seconds longer, then got up and sat at the table. Still stunned with the change in my mother, I began arranging my school work and looking at what kind of mess the cereal caused. I wondered briefly if she was going to come back in the kitchen and attack me again, but I heard her dialing on the phone. *I only have to put up with this for one more month*, I reminded myself. *Vickie just has to sign the lease on the apartment. One more month.* I started drawing things that looked like science and math formulas but that were really just gibberish. My hands were shaking horribly and I tried to make them stop but they wouldn't. In the living room, my mother was talking on the phone. I didn't know who she was talking to.

"He said he wanted to fuck me," she said. "Can you believe such a thing?"

I wanted to run in there and tell her how stupid she was, that she couldn't even figure out what I had said, but instead I drew more squiggles that looked like math equations. (Now, I wonder if she had understood me but was lying to the person on the other line in hope of gaining some sympathy. I also often wonder how the person reacted.) I remembered having hit my mother's breasts and remembered how close our bodies had been when we were fighting on the floor. I didn't form an actual thought, but I didn't want to talk about any of it, so I gathered my books and papers and went to my room. My mother was still talking. I could hear her through the thin walls. I lay down in my clothes without turning the light off.

I divided thirty days by two and got fifteen. I divided fifteen by one-half and got thirty. Three times zero, and got zero. I smiled at the thought. I divided three by zero and closed my eyes, trying to remember the smells of Richmond, the taste of McDonald's hamburgers, the busy-ness of the college campus. I ran through the comic book characters I could be and decided again on the Hulk. I felt the change coming on and welcomed the surge of strength the transformation would bring.

Stacey Richter

Barbie vs. Stalin

In the matter of Barbie v. Stalin, a troika of judges will render a final decision. They will be protected by a cloak of anonymity for obvious reasons.

Exhibit A: Barbie
Barbie was created in 1959. Her architect, Ruth Handler, observed her daughter dressing paper dolls and theorized that little girls might enjoy playing with a doll that looked like a grown woman rather than like a baby. Executives at Mattel were not impressed by the idea, but by then Handler had discovered the example of Bild Lilli, a wildly popular German doll with an hourglass figure. Bild Lilli was based on a character from a newspaper cartoon, a ditzy, sexpot secretary who was always on the lookout for a rich man to fund her all-night partying. She made quips like: "I could do without the balding old men but my budget couldn't!" Barbie and Bild Lilli share many physical characteristics, including long legs, a wasp waist, and a strange, sidelong glance (Barbie's eyes were straightened in the early 1970's). The Lilli doll, unlike Barbie, was originally intended for the adult market (she was sold in bars and tobacco shops); however, little girls took to her right away and she had long since become a popular plaything in Germany before Mattel acquired her rights and ceased her production in 1964.

Barbie, on the other hand, was always meant to be a toy. She was originally marketed as Barbie the Teen-Age Fashion Model, but despite her youth and apparent virginity, her wild curves reveal the submerged spirit of Bild Lilli, a girl who is at best a sassy opportunist and at worst a prostitute.

Since then, Barbie has become one of the most popular toys of all times and a pop culture icon. Over the years she's been widely criticized for presenting an unrealistic vision of femininity—if she were human, her body fat would be so low that she'd be unable to menstruate. (The 1965 Slumber Party Barbie came with a diet book that contained the advice, "Don't eat!" and a scale that read 110, making her about 35 pounds underweight for a woman of Barbie's height, expanded to human scale.) This criticism seems strange since the whole point of Barbie is that she presents an unrealistic view of femininity. Barbie is a talisman, a symbol of sexiness, an embodiment of the human urge to exaggerate virtue that's seen in examples as disparate as the poetry of Homer, GI Joe, and the Venus of Willendorf, the ancient, softball-sized fertility symbol, who, with her giant breasts and huge ass, could arguably be called Barbie's rightful mother.

To counter the criticism of Barbie's physique, Mattel widened Barbie's waist and has given her an endless parade of "jobs" over the years, including paleontologist, McDonald's cashier, NASCAR driver, and dentist (there is no Call Girl Barbie, perhaps because every Barbie is Call Girl Barbie). In any case, Barbie is not a constant object in the physical sense. She has sported various physical permutations, including hair that grows from a spool when her belly is pressed, arms that shimmy when a lever is wiggled, and breast plate that snaps opens like a locket to reveal a pot of lip gloss (in the body of a blonde Barbie), or a photo of blonde Barbie (in the body of the brunette).

Barbie is still one of the world's most popular toys, though in recent years she's lost ground to the competing line of Bratz dolls. Bratz, with their swollen, anime-style eyes, long hair, and skimpy costumes, are even more whorish in appearance than Barbie, who has increasingly been dressing in princess ball gowns or sporty, practical gear appropriate to her professional status. Barbie has a stiff opponent in Bratz, who is plainly cast from the same mold as Bild Lilli—a sexy, underemployed, shopping-crazed tart.

In response to the Bratz threat, Mattel has made Barbie's head bigger.

Exhibit B: Stalin
Stalin was born in 1878 in Gori, Georgia. His father was a cobbler and an alcoholic who eventually drank himself to death; his mother took in sewing and probably slept with her employers in exchange for money and favors. In Gori, a rough and tumble town full of ruffians, Stalin's father was known for his particularly brutal beatings of his wife and son.

During his youth, despite the protectiveness of his mother, Stalin was twice struck by horse-drawn carriages and sustained lasting damage to his left arm. He walked with a limp and contracted smallpox when he was seven, which left his face heavily scarred. Official photographs were always retouched.

Though his family was poor, they managed to send Stalin (whose real name was Iosif Vissarionovich Dzhugashvili) to seminary schools, where the priests surveilled and harassed their charges, hoping to keep them from girls, wine, self-abuse, and the forbidden revolutionary texts that were in vogue at the time. Though clearly this persecution had the opposite effect than the one intended (shortly before graduation, Stalin dropped out of school to become a revolutionary), some have attributed Stalin's invention of the terror state to the incessant spying on the part of the priests, who tirelessly violated their students privacy. It was not unusual for teachers at the seminary to paw through their charge's dirty laundry.

Stalin himself seemed more impressed by the tactics of Hitler, who pitted one faction of followers against the other in the Night of the Long Knives (when the leaders of the SA were accused of fictional crimes and shot by the Gestapo). By then, of course, Stalin had become the General Secretary of the Communist Party's Central Committee, the defacto ruler of the Soviet Union, having consolidated his power through canny maneuvering that pitted his rivals against each other. He made good use of false charges and threats and later, when he was more powerful, of forced confessions and the firing squad. He had a dead-on skill for manipulation—not, presumably, based on charm, which, with his heavy Georgian accent, course ways, and short stature, many denied—but rather, based on a total lack of allegiance or sympathy for others that is difficult to comprehend. Though he was sentimental, he had no fixed loyalties. By the end of his life he'd turned against nearly all of his friends; of the six members of the original Politburo who lived until the Great Purge, only Stalin survived. His second wife committed suicide over his policies, not to mention his cruel treatment of her (he flicked cigarettes at her during a state dinner). He rarely saw his children though he took pains to be sure they received no special treatment. When his son attempted suicide and failed, Stalin is said to have remarked: "You can't even do that right."

By many estimates Stalin is responsible for the death of 20 million people, perhaps even more, though he only had about 700,000 shot directly. The others died in the Gulag, in transport, or as a result of famine due to his directive, issued at the dawn of farm collectivization, to confiscate every last grain of wheat from the countryside. During the Great Purge, roughly half of the Soviet political and military establishment was executed or imprisoned, along with hundreds of thousands of citizens who were almost randomly accused—through forced confessions, bitterness, personal ambition, or for no reason at all—of anti-Soviet activity, spying, or wrecking.

Stalin is perhaps the most ruthless and murderous human of recorded history. It's unclear why he was so brutal. Human psychology does not extend to one willing and able to exist outside of all constraints and morality, both inner and outer. When Stalin's comrade Bukharin was sentenced to death, he sent a note that said, "Koba, why do you need me to die?" This is known because after Stalin's own death, the note was found in his desk. He'd kept it, presumably, as a souvenir: a sort of sentimental reminder of his friend, the affection between them (the nickname "Koba"), and a reminder of how he'd had him executed. The meaning of this memento is unclear because there's nothing to compare it to; almost no one else would ever be in the position to procure such a thing, let alone make it a keepsake.

A few additional facts: Stalin gave himself the name Stalin, which means "man of steel." His grandparents were serfs. *Time* magazine twice named him Man of the Year. He had a taste for young girls and fathered two children with a thirteen year-old. Two toes of his left foot were webbed. In his youth, he was known for his lovely singing voice.

Though Stalin installed his mother in a former castle in Gori, he avoided visiting her for many years. When she fell ill and he went to see her at last, the doctor who was treating her reported this odd conversation:

Stalin: "Mother why did you beat me so hard?"

Keke: "That's why you turned out so well." Then she asked, "Joseph, who exactly are you now?"

Stalin: "Remember the tsar? Well, I'm like a tsar."
Keke: "You'd have done better to have become a priest."

The Opinions of the Judges

Judge A: The winner is Stalin. As the chief terrorist of the twentieth century, Stalin has left an indelible mark on history in general, the former Soviet Union specifically, and in the lives of countless individuals. His legacy reverberates in a host of strong, crafty, manipulative leaders as diverse as Kim Jong-il, Vladimir Putin, and Dick Cheney. His example of rule through might, propaganda, and deviousness—not to mention his industrialization of the Soviet Union, leading directly to the Cold War—ushered in our current modern age of cynicism, fear, and a total lack of idealism. Even if Stalin is no longer the Man of the Year, the specter of a paternalistic ruler who is covertly evil is the dominant figure of our times as represented in film, life, and the dreams of countless individuals. Also, he defeated Hitler.

Judge B: The weight of industrial stagnation, empty propaganda, and suppressed nationalism probably would not have sunk the Soviet Union without a population that had a keening and unanswered desire for consumer goods. And what is Barbie if not a consumer good? She who is herself the tiniest consumer? Empires may come and go but the lust for material objects—particularly an object who herself embodies lust—is constant. In a war between ideologies, the best is one that is unrecognized, an ideology so ubiquitous that it's casually proclaimed by all, from every direction, and is perceived as such a given that it is incapable of being unmasked. For evidence of the supremacy of Barbie and all she stands for, just ask any beautiful sorority girl if she thinks she's fat. The answer is yes and the winner is Barbie.

Judge C: I agree with judge B.

The winner is Barbie.

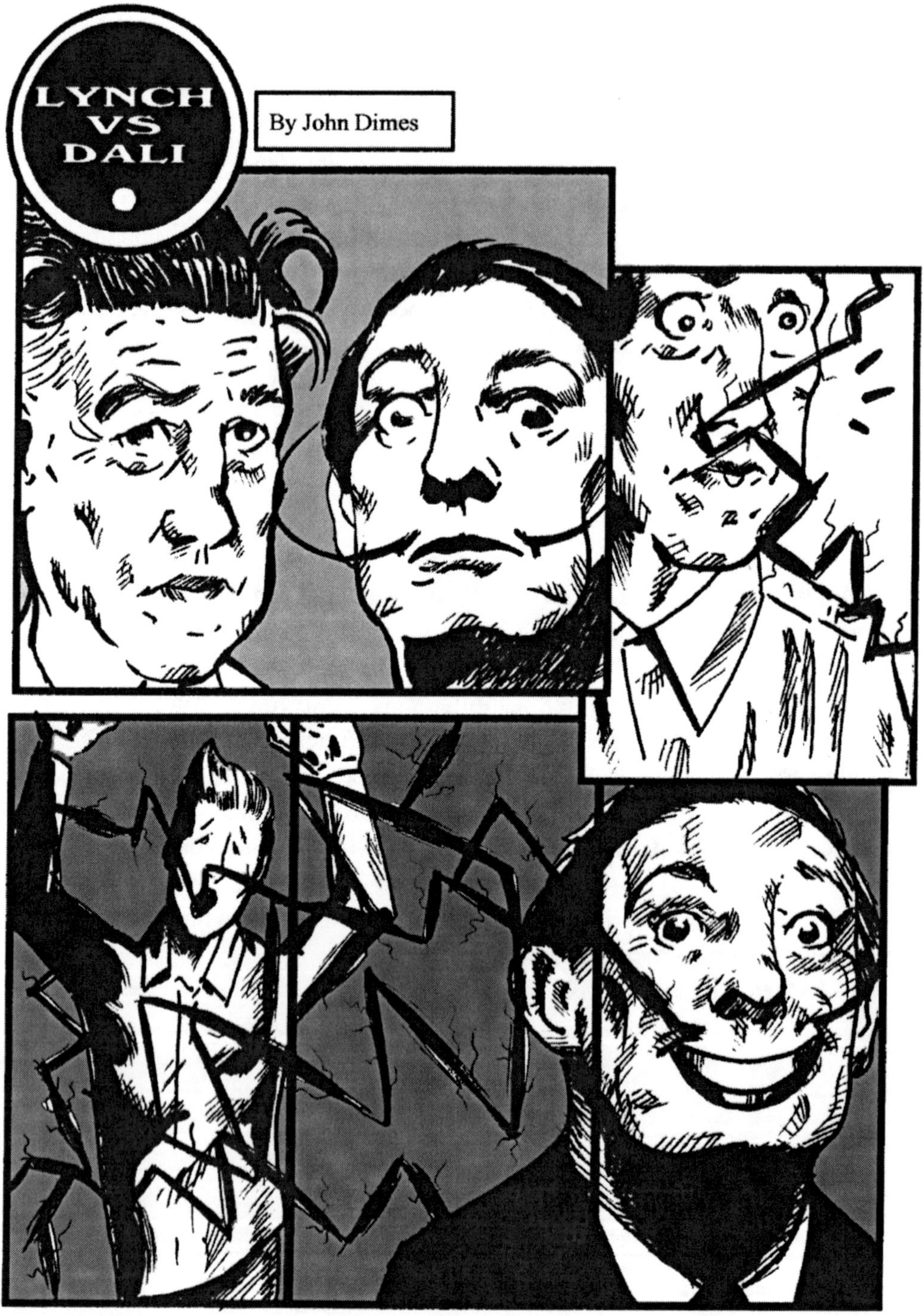
LYNCH
VS
DALI
By John Dimes

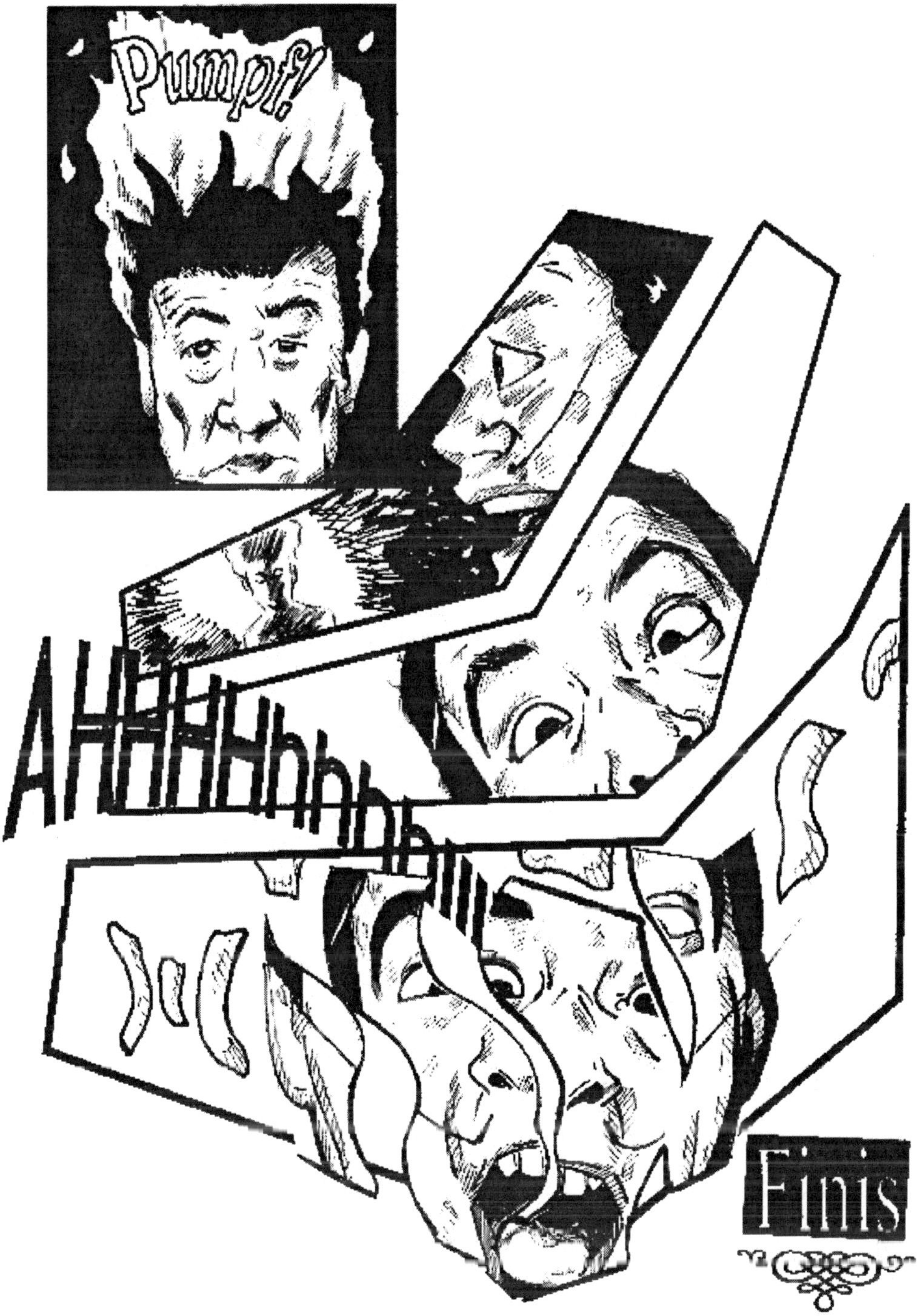
Pumpf!
AHHHHhhhh!!!
Finis

Laura Benedict

Love vs. Lust

Lust pierced the veil separating her from the children of Adam, touching them with her face, her palms and fingers, causing their skin to ripple and shiver, distracting them from their Noble Thoughts.

"Stop it!" Love reached out from where he reclined nearby, but didn't try to touch her. He wasn't sure what would happen to him if his skin were to finally meet hers. Dishonor? Death? Disease? He'd watched her consume the children of Adam, the ones who had fallen against the veil, joyfully rending it, the ones who had felt her touch and embraced it. He'd seen Lust's enormous mouth—all wet-shined lips and muscled tongue and glittering saliva—stretch open so that the children of Adam would tumble inside to drown. Sometimes he dreamed that he was a child of Adam who had succumbed, falling into the wet cave of her mouth, falling down, down into the inner expanse of her taut but generous belly where the vile delights of the ones who had gotten there before him thrilled and sickened him. But he always forced himself awake from the dream, remembering it was nothing more than an Ignoble Thought.

Still, he loved her because it was his nature to love. Still, he wondered what it would be like to touch her. To *be* her.

"You're no fun," Lust said, drawing back so that a child of Adam, no longer sustained by her caress, fell back and crawled away. Love watched after him until he rose and walked, unsteady, and Love said a silent prayer of thanks.

Lust climbed up onto her bier, arranging her mass of curls around her shoulders so that they wouldn't obscure the row of breasts above her belly. Seeing Love watching her, she laughed and curved her fingers around her middle breast and squeezed. A single amber pearl seemed to grow from the nipple. When Lust touched the pearl it melted onto her fingertip, and she held it out to him.

"Taste," she said.

Love was hungry, but he turned his face away, overcome. Why was it that when he wasn't looking at her he imagined her to be enormous, frightening—a well-cushioned Valkyrie, a creature with more arms than even breasts, arms that might enfold and crush him? But when he looked back at her he saw that she was lush and pink with health, not at all larger than he; she held her two supple but otherwise ordinary arms out to him, fingers fluid and beckoning, the drop glistening at the tip of a forefinger.

He felt the great heat that burned inside her as she opened her mouth and touched her finger to her tongue. The drop spread over the red and mottled surface like warm honey. Tasting it, her eyes lost their focus and then she closed them.

Love wondered at her momentary pleasure. He'd witnessed her tantrums, the way she thrashed in her sleep, heard the cries of the children of Adam from deep in her belly, and knew she lived at the mercy of the endless needs of her body. He pitied her.

"I think the heat inside of you is killing you, Lust," he said. "Come here so I can cool you off."

Lust sighed, falling back onto the bier's nest of aubergine pillows. "You think too much, Love."

"You want too much, Lust. You're never content to just exist." He smiled at her to let her know he felt compassion for her, that he wasn't cruel.

"Kingdoms have been built on these lips," Lust said. She kissed her fingers and blew the kiss to him on a soft breeze. A pulsing wreath of light and shadow shimmered in the air for a moment, then burst into a million grains of color, the same iridescent green and gold of Lust's eyes. As it disappeared it left behind the scents of tuberose and animal sweat, which, rather than repelling Love, caused the hunger in his belly to sharpen.

"And from here." Lust touched her fingers to the glistening mound of tight golden curls between her legs and moved them in a slow, deliberate circle.

To anyone else, Lust might have seemed mad. Beyond redemption. But Love was patient. He thought he might teach her.

"And from here," he said, resting a hand on the flesh covering his heart, for he was naked as well.

"Pah!" Lust said, sitting up. The veil clung to her in places, undulating with the constant passing of the children of Adam, but she ignored it. "Name one."

"Victoria and Albert," Love said.

"No fair, she had the kingdom already," Lust said.

Love was amused by the petulant turn of her lips. He wondered what they tasted like.

"Abram and Sarai," Love said. "You can't argue with that kingdom."

"Took him a few tries," Lust said. "And Hagar wasn't complaining." She absentmindedly toyed with her leftmost nipple, causing a thin stream of milk to wind its way down the curve of her breast and drip with exquisite slowness onto her belly. Love's mouth went dry as he imagined climbing onto her bier and licking the milk from her flesh.

"If you're going to go all biblical on me, what about David and Bathsheba?" she said. "And Jezebel and Ahab. Major horndog, that Ahab."

"Odysseus and Penelope," Love said.

"No kingdom," Lust said. "Who knows if he was lying? There were a lot of years in between."

"Catherine and Heathcliff," Love said, clutching his side. The hunger in his gut felt vast, as though it could never be filled.

"What is it?" Lust said. "What's wrong?"

For the briefest of moments he imagined that he saw pain and worry in her eyes. But he knew it was a parody of true concern. He knew concern. Lust knew Other Things. But wasn't it the purview of Love to know All Things?

"You might help me," he said, doubling over. What a shameful ruse! Who knew he was capable of such duplicity?

"I might," she said. Her voice was shy.

He watched her diminutive, perfectly-formed feet as she slipped from the bier. A bit of the veil caught and clung to her heel and she tried to kick it away, but it held fast. Love had never touched the veil.

Her heat came to him slowly; her weak cry revealed that everything she touched absorbed her, took her essence, draining her. He hadn't noticed it before, when she touched the children of Adam. Or was it only he who harmed her?

Then her hands were on him, and again he felt like there were a hundred of them; they covered his body, kneading his cold flesh, suffusing it with warmth like he'd never known before. Her hair draped over him like a stole, crept between their lips and into his mouth.

But if you bite and devour one another, take heed that you be not consumed one of another.

All his fear had gone, leaving hunger in its place.

Her lips!

At the union of their lips, the heat and the cool met in equal measure. Her mouth, which had seemed enormous and threatening to him now seemed small. He covered her lips with his own, then stretched them further, further over the roses of her cheeks and cherubic chin, and her startled eyes. Her head, with its golden curls, almost filled him—but he swallowed, opening for her, letting her fall deep, deep inside him. He relished the curves of her waist and sturdy fingertips and the breadth of her bright pink thighs. When he came to her feet, the veil clung to his lip.

Finally, he was satisfied. Pulling the veil gently from him, he smoothed it where it hung and stepped around it to walk among the children of Adam.

Becky Hagenston

Dorothy Gale vs. Alice Liddell

A girl couldn't stay here forever, in a podunk town in the middle of nowhere, and thank God Jason agreed with her. Dorothy had convinced him to marry her as soon as she turned sixteen, and they would take the train to Omaha or Kansas City or maybe even Chicago. Ever since the storm last year, and the dream-that-wasn't-a-dream, she had been restless, as if her heart had been set spinning and spinning and hadn't stopped, might never stop. Her uncle said it was hormones. Her aunt had given her a book called *What's Happening to Me?*—really written for much younger children, but better late than never. "If you have any questions," her aunt said, then turned crimson and rushed down the hall to check on her apple pie.

Dorothy had started wearing her crisp blouse tied at the midriff. She cut her hair into a dark bob with her aunt's sewing scissors. At night, she had dreams about Jason that woke her up with a crack of lightning in the lower, secret parts of herself. There was nothing in *What's Happening to Me?* that addressed this specifically.

At school she was more popular than unpopular, and kids hung around her lunch table to hear stories about the flying monkeys and the Emerald City and the melting witch and the hot air balloon. Her best friend Dana—whom Dorothy met when she used to go to 4-H—liked the story about the melting witch the best. Jason preferred the giant spider.

And then, last week, an exchange student named Alice had shown up, dressed in a pinafore like Dorothy used to wear, her hair tied in a bow, talking like the Queen of England. Dorothy hated her on sight, and hated her even more when she saw Alice at the preppy lunch table (it figured) surrounded not only by preppies, but Goths and Jocks, too. Dorothy got close enough to hear her saying, "And then when I ate it, I grew and grew! It was very curious!"

Dorothy didn't think it was curious at all, but she still hung around long enough to hear Alice go on about some talking Dodo—which was bullshit, everyone knew they were extinct—and then she saw Jason, *her* Jason, leaning toward that British tart, his eyes as round as tea saucers.

Alice was living with the Hausers, a farming family who couldn't have children of their own and apparently thought the next best thing was importing a pinafore-wearing crumpet-eater.

"She's actually really fascinating." This came from Dana, one afternoon at Dana's barn. Dorothy still sometimes helped Dana feed the chickens, if she could do it from enough of a distance not to get her slippers dirty. "She once stepped through a mirror into a land of talking chess pieces. It's no Emerald City!" Dana added hastily. "But it's cool. I like her accent."

Dorothy tossed chicken feed into Dana's face and went home.

"She's okay," Jason said, at the lockers between fifth and sixth periods. He shrugged and wouldn't look Dorothy in the eye.

Dorothy stomped her feet. "She's *not* okay," she said, and was mortified to realize her eyes were filling with tears. Today she was wearing her shirt tied up even higher than usual, and her uncle had frowned at her as she left the house. Jason didn't seem to care.

It was Dana who told Dorothy what was going to happen on Saturday afternoon: Alice and Jason were going to meet up in Jason's storm cellar. "Just for tea, though," Dana insisted. "That's what Alice told me. Tea and chess." Really, Dana was one of the most naïve idiots Dorothy had ever known, stupider than a brainless scarecrow.

"Thanks," said Dorothy.

"Don't do anything," Dana warned, and Dorothy said, "Right."

They didn't hear her come down the wooden steps of the storm cellar, didn't notice her at all because—as Dorothy had suspected—they weren't playing chess *or* drinking tea, though the pieces were set out neatly on the board, next to a bone china tea set.

Jason's hand was up Alice's dress and Alice had her hand on his neck, murmuring, *Eat me, drink me, oh yes, please.*

Dorothy stood motionless for a moment, as hot and cold forces collided within her (She loved him! She *didn't* love him!) and set her tornado heart spinning free.

The Mason jars of preserves went first—splat against the wall—then the peaches, then the beans. She grabbed a jug of water and flung it against the concrete floor and laughed as it exploded. She whirled and whirled, laughing, tossing jars of pickles, maple syrup, apple butter, then pinging the chess pieces against the wall (Alice and Jason cowered, then ran, not that Dorothy noticed), then the bone china tea set with dainty red roses—crushed and shattered, the shards disintegrating beneath Dorothy's slippers as she spun and spun, a force of nature, until there was nothing left to smash and she slowed down, flushed and dizzy.

When she caught her breath, she hardly knew where she was.

The next day, Jason apologized but she shrugged him off. She was beyond Jason now, Jason was a speck in a haystack she was soaring over.

Alice never returned to school. The heartbroken Hausers found a note on their kitchen table, informing them that she was taking a cab to the airport. America was too curious for her, she wrote, and there was no place like home.

K. H. Solomon

Fighting Bull

His fine and fearsome form embodies Wild.
The ivory horns arch gracefully in space,
their tapered shapes spread out, curve front, and curve
again in gentle rise to lethal tip.
He has his father's mighty neck°, whose hump
will gorge on blood and swell when he's enraged,
a massive chest and muscled shoulders, stacked
on short quick stubs of legs with cloven hooves.

His coat is black, matte black — so black it seems
his teeth must surely be black onyx,
his moist warm fetid breath must reek of char,
and even must his mother's heart° pump dark
red viscous blood in surges through his veins.
His open gaze befits immortal beast:
no airs to show he has no fear at death,
for in him neither fear nor death is known.

To see, up close, this mythic monster, both
destroyer and creator, is to know
the awe of ancient men who fought the bull
and painted walls of caves, to know that it
takes all that men with horses, lances, capes
and swords, and reverence through millennia
can do to kill him, if indeed they can
— and to know that even so he lives.

° Breeders of fighting bulls believe a bull inherits his size and strength from his father, but his courage, will and fighting spirit from his mother.

Josh Woods

JESUS VS. THOR

Now it came to pass, under the sign of Pisces, that a vision was opened & was given.
& Behold:

Along the red & cloudy wastes of Jupiter marched an army & their number was 144,000 & each soldier brandished an unblemished spear & wore a vestment of bronze & each grew a narrow beard like unto a pillar of stone & each soldier upon his forehead did two names gleam like fire & these two names were

יהושע & יהוה

Each soldier was a virgin & was angry.
The army of 144,000 did clutch their spears & sing a hymn mighty unlike any hymn & it was New to their Lord & all Lords.
Thus did they provoke a jealousy.

The red & cloudy wastes of Jupiter did splash aside to a racing chariot. 2 black goats pulled the chariot & their names were Tooth-Gnasher & Gap-Tooth. Aloft in the chariot stood a mighty figure who was called Ása-Thór & his beard was like unto a fiery mane of a lion & iron gauntlets weighed on his mighty hands & a belt of strength did skirt his waist like unto a fortress wall & raised above his head he held a horrid hammer which was wicked, which was ancient, upon which were engraved 3 terrible secrets which no god could decipher & all who are well-informed of this hammer call it only Mjöllnir.

Then Ása-Thór did speak with his mighty voice:
>—By what authority does this army sing a New praise where mine ears may hear it? For there will be trouble!

Then the black goats Tooth-Gnasher & Gap-Tooth chomped their jaws like thunder & Ása-Thór rode without fear through the centre of the army of 144,000 & he bore down on them with tremendous speed & he swung Mjöllnir across their ranks & the heads of the army of 144,000 did toss like unto a reaping of grain & did splatter like unto grapes of the vine. The song of the army of 144,000 did stop & only did they wail & flee. But Ása-Thór chased them in his chariot for sport & smashed their heads & he laughed & the laugh of Ása-Thór did sound as this:
>—Hor hor hor hor hor hor hor hor hor hor hor hor hor hor hor hor hor hor hor hor hor hor hor hor hor hor hor hor hor hor hor hor hor! Hor!

& it was then that the army of 144,000 which was now the army of 48,621 did stop fleeing & grow silent. Likewise did Ása-Thór furrow his brow & become silent.

The red & cloudy wastes of Jupiter were disturbed & stirred & obscured because of the massacre of the army of 48,621.

Then through the bloody mist strode a strange shape. It did hobble on 4 hooves & did bleed from the neck like unto a river & it became clear to all that it was the Lamb.

& the Lamb was a terrible sight to behold. 7 crooked horns did protrude from its skull & 7 blank eyes did scatter its face & dark blood did cake its torn wool & all who are well-informed of this Lamb know that it had been slaughtered. But it hobbled toward Ása-Thór.

& the army of forty-eight-thousand-six-hundred-twenty-one did call its name:
>—Yeshua Mshicha! Yeshua bin Yahweh!

Then did Ása-Thór snort his nostrils & hurl Mjöllnir at the Lamb. Mjöllnir gleamed like lightning as it tumbled across the red & cloudy wastes of Jupiter & it crashed into the skull of the Lamb & shattered 2 of its horns & put out 3 of its eyes & snapped its neck to its shoulder & cleaved its skull & the Lamb fell to its side.

& the Lamb was dead.

Then did Ása-Thór step down from his chariot with much pleasure & he did pat the heads of his 2 goats Tooth-Gnasher & Gap-Tooth & with his iron gauntlets he did lift corpses by the number of 9 at a time in each hand & did pile them so as to make a pyre to commemorate his glory.

The army of 48,621 watched in horror & prayed for their destroyed soldiers.

Ása-Thór did throw the corpses in a pile that was 82 cubits wide & did throw the corpses atop each other until the pile was 359 cubits high & all who are well-informed of this tower of corpses know that it was tall & vast & terrible. Then did Ása-Thór behold his labors & speak:

—The tips of Yggdrasil are challenged by this heavy work!

The last corpse to be pilled atop the tower of corpses was that of the Lamb, but as Ása-Thór strode near the Lamb, the Lamb did wobble to its feet.

The neck of the Lamb was still broken to its side & the horns of the Lamb were still shattered & the eyes of the Lamb were still put out & the neck of the Lamb did still bleed as a river, but the Lamb stood.

This did greatly anger Ása-Thór & he spoke:

—This greatly angers me! For there will be now the most trouble!

& the countenance of Ása-Thór did seem to grow like unto a thunderhead & Ása-Thór clutched the Lamb by the wool with his iron fingers & spun his feet in a violent circle & became a whirlwind & released the Lamb & the Lamb did fly far out of sight across the red & cloudy wastes of Jupiter.

But Ása-Thór saw that in his palm which had clutched the thick wool of the Lamb there were scattered wax crumbs of a broken seal. Ása-Thór licked them off his gauntlet & spit them out again because the taste did not please him.

Then did cry out the army of 48,621:

—Behold! The White Horse approacheth!

& there rode forth a White Horse upon which sat a White Rider who held a long White bow & who wore a tall White crown & who wore a White veil over his face & who did sing in a most beautiful voice:

> —I come forth conquering & to conquer! I come forth conquering & to conquer! I come forth conquering & to conquer!

At this, Ása-Thór did not stoop to retrieve Mjöllnir for he was jolly & he ran forth toward the rider at tremendous speed & his feet did quake the red & cloudy wastes of Jupiter & he spread his arms & did speak:

> —That I should embrace this conqueror!

Straightaway did the White Rider upon the White Horse & Ása-Thór clash so that the heavens did rumble. Ása-Thór pressed against the White Horse breast to breast & did clasp his iron gauntlets at the rump of the White Horse & did lift the White Horse & squeeze it terribly.

The White Rider nocked a thin White arrow & pulled his long White bow & shot it down at the face of Ása-Thór like unto a beam of light.

Ása-Thór dropped the White Horse from his grip & clutched his eyes & screeched out of his throat & the screech of Ása-Thór did sound like the screech of a woman.

It was then that the river of blood that had been left from the neck of the Lamb did pool at the base of the tower of corpses since they did weigh down the red & cloudy wastes of Jupiter. The corpses began to twitch & splash in the blood of the Lamb & the corpses at the bottom of the tower of corpses drank the blood of the Lamb deeply & like unto a fountain the blood of the Lamb flowed upward through the tower for they were One. The tower of corpses began to sway & groan. & one by one the corpse arms which brandished spears did stretch out at every side of the tower of corpses. Feet of the corpses stood at the base to lift the tower of corpses & it was like unto a tall nation of tight dead & the thousands of indignant eyes did look toward Ása-Thór

& the tower of corpses lurched toward Ása-Thór.

& the army of 48,621 fell into ranks behind the White Rider upon the White Horse. & the White Rider sang for a volley of spears toward Ása-Thór.

& they were tossed. The flock of spears climbed high & blackened the heavens & tilted down & rained upon the back of Ása-Thór. Every spear of the army of 48,621 did pierce Ása-Thór & his back was like unto a thick forest.

Ása-Thór stumbled to the selfsame spot where he had killed the Lamb & the legs of Ása-Thór shuddered & he fell to his knees.

The tower of corpses lumbered toward the fallen form of Ása-Thór & trampled over him & did retract their feet & the tower of corpses dropped onto Ása-Thór & crushed him & the tower of corpses did sway mightily & did groan mightily.

& from over the horizon of the red & cloudy wastes of Jupiter did the Lamb come a-tromping. The front leg of the Lamb was broken & did show a sharp bone protruding & the Lamb fell each time on this leg as it tromped & the head of the Lamb hung by a string of flesh & the head did flop as the Lamb tromped & blood poured from its neck like unto a river & the hooves of the Lamb did slip as it tromped. Yet the Lamb came a-tromping.

& the White Rider upon the White Horse & the army of forty-eight-thousand-six-hundred-twenty-one & the tower of corpses all rejoiced at this sight & they did sing the mighty hymn which was unlike any hymn & which was New to their Lord & all Lords.

The Lamb was among them & tried to stand on its broken leg which would not hold steady. All raised their palms high & continued to rejoice around the Lamb.

But the music of the hymn that was New was disturbed by a single voice. & all who were singing looked over their shoulders & did quiet their singing, but they could not find the voice that disturbed their hymn that was New.

Then the red & cloudy wastes of Jupiter began to churn & rumble & storm. The hymn of all did fall to silence. The voice was muffled but began to grow clear & the voice came from the base of the tower of corpses & all who are well-informed know that the voice was not of madness alone, nor of fey alone, nor of vengeance alone, nor of blood-thirst alone. The voice was that which can no longer be understood because it came from an age that is no more.

It was the voice of a warrior & it did say this:

—FOR WRATH! FOR GLORY!

The tower of corpses did shake. The tower of corpses did lift. The tower of corpses balanced on the back of Ása-Thór who grit his teeth &

strained his legs & gnarled his face & gripped in both of his iron gauntlets the horrid hammer Mjöllnir.

& Ása-Thór was screaming!

Ása-Thór swung Mjöllnir above him & struck the tower of corpses that weighed on his back & a great crack split up the tower of corpses like unto lightning. Ása-Thór steadied Mjöllnir again & struck again & the tower of corpses did explode & did shatter & there was a rain of meat upon the red & cloudy wastes of Jupiter & the rain had no end.

& Ása-Thór was screaming!

Ása-Thór raised Mjöllnir aloft & charged the White Rider upon the White Horse & the ranks of the army of 48,621. But the ranks did scatter & flee & wail in terror at the sight of Ása-Thór.

& Ása-Thór was screaming!

The White Rider upon the White Horse nocked a thin White arrow with his graceful hand & released it toward Ása-Thór, but Ása-Thór caught the arrow in the air with his iron gauntlet & crushed the arrow like unto a sliver of ice. Then Ása-Thór bore down upon the White Rider upon the White Horse & swung Mjöllnir which did cave into the skull of the White Horse through its neck down to its shoulder & the White Horse did fall dead. The White Rider did scurry away, but Ása-Thór caught him up by his tall White crown & tossed him to the ground. Then Ása-Thór stomped his boot on the chest of the White Rider & did watch his ribs split & his lungs flatten & his heart pop.

& Ása-Thór was screaming!

& Ása-Thór stomped hard with his boot again & again & again & again & again & again

& again & again until the corpse of the
White

Rider was one with the rain of meat that did not end.

Then Ása-Thór did stop & did glare at the Lamb & did breathe loudly with his nostrils.

The head of the Lamb which hung by a string of flesh did stare at Ása-Thór with 4 blank eyes & 3 eyes that were put out.

Ása-Thór did see that the Lamb wavered where it stood & he strode to the Lamb slowly & lifted the horrid hammer Mjöllnir above his head & Ása-Thór asked the Lamb a question:

—Do you wish to speak a final curse? For I promise I will promptly kill you.

& the jaws of the Lamb did open & as the Lamb spoke & the Words of the Lamb were Holy that they did forge a gleaming sword from its tongue. & the tongue of the Lamb was Holy & the gleaming sword was Holy.

& Ása-Thór grabbed the blade of the gleaming sword with his iron gauntlet & ripped it out of the mouth of the Lamb & dashed it underfoot. Then he brought down Mjöllnir with the mightiest swing onto the spine of the Lamb & knocked the Lamb through the surface of the red & cloudy wastes of Jupiter through the hot core of the planet to the other side & the Lamb left only an abysmal hole in its wake.

Ása-Thór leapt into the abysmal hole to chase the corpse of the Lamb to collect a trophy from the remains of the Lamb & Ása-Thór did fall through the hot core of the planet & did fall out of the abysmal hole on the other side of the red & cloudy wastes of Jupiter & there did find the Lamb in shambles with shreds of flesh clinging to its bones which were exposed & its blood was spreading like unto a lake.

But the Lamb did stumble to its feet. Again.

& at this sight Ása-Thór was filled with a great fury & he was dizzy & he did scream words which were this:

—Then I will eat you!

& Ása-Thór waded through the lake of the blood of the Lamb & did gather the pieces of the Lamb into the palms of his iron gauntlets & did shove the Lamb into his mighty mouth.

& Ása-Thór chomped his mighty teeth.

Inside the world of the mouth of Ása-Thór, the tongue did push the flesh around like unto an dusky tide & the ivory mountains which hung in the heavens crashed down & rose again & crashed down again & crushed all the bones of the Lamb & broke all the horns of the Lamb & smashed all the eyes of the Lamb & ground all the organs of the Lamb. The vast pit of the throat swallowed the flesh of the Lamb & drank the blood of the Lamb.

& all fell into the mighty stomach of Ása-Thór.

Inside the world of the stomach of Ása-Thór, all was without form & was void. Darkness was upon the face of the deep. & From the body of the Lamb, a light grew & did grow. & the light changed all things & all things were forever changed.

Contributors

Joshua Archer studied fine art and played football at the University of Toledo, and his work is on permanent exhibition at the university and throughout the city. He is now at work with Kyle Minor on a book-length version of Else Richter's story.

Laura Benedict is the author of the novels *Isabella Moon* and *Calling Mr. Lonely Hearts*. Her fiction has appeared in *Ellery Queen Mystery Magazine* and other anthologies, and she has worked for the past decade as a freelance book reviewer for *The Grand Rapids Press* and other newspapers. She edits the anthology series *Surreal South* with her husband Pinckney Benedict.

Pinckney Benedict grew up on his family's dairy farm in southern West Virginia. He has published two collections of short fiction (*Town Smokes* and *The Wrecking Yard*) and a novel (*Dogs of God*). His stories have appeared in a number of magazines and anthologies, including *Esquire*, *Zoetrope: All-Story*, *StoryQuarterly*, *Ontario Review*, the *O. Henry Award* series, the *New Stories from the South* series, the *Pushcart Prize* series, and *The Oxford Book of American Short Stories*. He is the editor, along with his wife, the novelist Laura Benedict, of the 2007 anthology *Surreal South* (also from Press53), which promises to be the first in an ongoing biennial series. His honors and awards include a Literature Fellowship from the National Endowment for the Arts, a Literary Fellowship from the West Virginia Commission on the Arts, a Michener Fellowship from the Writers' Workshop at the University of Iowa, the Chicago Tribune's Nelson Algren Award, an Individual Artist grant from the Illinois Arts Council, and Britain's Steinbeck Award. He serves as a professor in the English Department at Southern Illinois University in Carbondale, Illinois. 'Orgo VS the Flatlanders' is his first illustrated fiction, and first appeared in the 2009 *Idaho Review*.

John Dimes is an artist and is the author of several books, including the Young Adult Fantasy novel *The Rites of Pretending Tribe* (Zumaya Publications) and the Dark Urban Fantasy *Intracations* (Darkhart Press). His shorter works have appeared in several magazines and anthologies which include *The Sound of Horror* (Magus Press); *Diabolic Tales: An Anthology of Dark Minds* (Diabolic Publications); *Read Your Fears* (Tricorner Publishing), and *Tales of the Slug* (Windstorm Creative). Visit his website at www.johndimes.com. See his insane promotional video for *Intracations* on youtube.com.

Okla Elliott is an Assistant Professor at Ohio Wesleyan University. He holds an MFA from Ohio State University and an MA from UNC-Greensboro. In addition to his American education, he has studied at the University of Mannheim, Germany, and at the University of Wroclaw, Poland. His non-fiction, poetry, short fiction, and translations have appeared or are forthcoming in *A Public Space, Blue Mesa Review, Cold Mountain Review, Indiana Review, International Poetry Review, Natural Bridge, New Letters, North Dakota Quarterly, Pedestal Magazine*, and the *Sewanee Theological Review*. He is the author of *The Mutable Wheel* and *Lucid Bodies and Other Poems*. He is also co-editor, with Kyle Minor, of *The Other Chekhov*.

El Pollo Diablo was the borned in a small fishing villages near the Mediteranean resort town of Cartegena in the late 16th century. Giving up the promising careers of being a cabana boy to the Spanish glitterati, he turned to a lifes of piracy, spreading fear and good fashion senses throughout the Carribbean. Now, nearly two hundred and fifty years after his untimely and bizarre deaths, involving an anchor chains, a feather pillow, a woman of leisure, and three coconuts, El Pollo Diablo occasionally materializes from the afterlifes to answer questions of the livings, and to spin wonderous tales full of hearty truthiness.

John Flaherty lives in Chicago. He is finishing his first novel, *Curse Keepers*, which chronicles the story of the secret organization determined to keep the Chicago Cubs from winning the World Series and, thereby, forestalling the end of the world.

Michael Garriga, a native of the Mississippi Gulf Coast, is currently a PhD candidate in Florida State University's creative writing program. He's published other duels in Black Warrior Review and Poetry Southeast, and now is completing a country noir novel.

Matthew Guenette's first book, *Sudden Anthem* (Dream Horse Press, 2008), won the 2007 American Poetry Journal Book Prize. His poems have been published in *Diagram, Pindeldyboz*, and the *Southern Indiana Review* among many others. He lives and works in Madison, WI.

Becky Hagenston's story collection, *A Gram of Mars*, won the 1997 Mary McCarthy Prize and was published by Sarabande Books. Her stories have appeared in *Southern Review, TriQuarterly, Gettysburg Review, Black Warrior Review, Freight Stories*, and many other journals, as well as the O. Henry anthology. She is an Associate Professor of English at Mississippi State University.

Michael Kimball's third novel, *Dear Everybody*, has just been published in the US, UK, and Canada (http://michael-kimball.com/). His first two novels are *The Way the Family Got Away* (2000) and *How Much of Us There Was* (2005), both of which have been translated (or are being translated) into many languages. He is also responsible for the collaborative art project—Michael Kimball Writes Your Life Story (on a postcard)—and the documentary film *I Will Smash You*.

Danielle Girard Kraus's novels include *Cold Silence*, winner of the 2002 Barry Award, and *Chasing Darkness*, which received an RT Reviewer's Choice Award. She is a graduate of the MFA program at Queens University in Charlotte, North Carolina; she and her family split their time between San Francisco and the Northern Rockies.

Alexander Lumans was born in Aiken, South Carolina, where, growing up, several children's books his parents read to him scarred him for life. His fiction has been published in *Clarkesworld*, and two of his book reviews have been published in the *Crab Orchard Review*. He recently won Honorable Mention in the 2008 Press53 Open Short Story contest, as well as a

Fellowship to study abroad in Galway, Ireland. Currently, he is enrolled in the MFA Fiction Program at Southern Illinois University of Carbondale.

Margaret McMullan has written five novels including *In My Mother's House* (Thomas Dunne/St. Martin's 2003), *When I Crossed No-Bob* (Houghton Mifflin 2007), and the upcoming YA novel *Cashay* (Houghton Mifflin 2009). Her work has appeared in *Glamour*, the *Chicago Tribune*, *Southern Accents*, the *Indianapolis Star*, *TriQuarterly*, *Michigan Quarterly Review*, *The Greensboro Review*, *The Southern California Anthology*, *Other Voices*, *Boulevard*, *Ploughshares*, *The Pinch*, and *The Sun*. Visit her website at www.margaretmcmullan.com.

John McNally is author of two novels, *The Book of Ralph* and *America's Report Card*, and two story collections, *Troublemaker* and *Ghosts of Chicago*. He's also edited six anthologies, most recently *Who Can Save Us Now?: Brand-New Superheroes and Their Amazing (Short) Stories*, co-edited with Owen King. A native of Burbank, Illinois, John now lives and works in North Carolina.

Kyle Minor is the author of *In the Devil's Territory*, a collection of short fiction, and co-editor of *The Other Chekhov*, a new selection of Anton Chekhov stories. His recent work appears in literary magazines (*The Southern Review*, *The Gettysburg Review*), lurid websites (*Plots with Guns*, *Dogzplot*), and print anthologies (*Random House's Twentysomething Essays by Twentysomething Writers*, *Surreal South*, *Best American Mystery Stories*.)

Stacey Richter is the author of two short story collections, *My Date with Satan* and *Twin Study*. Her stories have been widely anthologized and have won many prizes, including four Pushcart prizes and the National Magazine Award.

Andrew Scott is the author of *Modern Love*, a short story chapbook. His fiction and nonfiction appears in *Esquire*, *The Cincinnati Review*, *Indianapolis Monthly*, *Mid-American Review*, *The Writer's Chronicle*, *Writers Ask*, and *Glimmer Train Stories*. He teaches writing at Ball State

University and lives in Indianapolis with his wife, the writer Victoria Barrett, where they edit *Freight Stories* (www.freightstories.com), an online fiction quarterly.

Curtis Smith's most recent novel is *Sound + Noise* (Casperian Books). His story collection *The Species Crown* was released by Press 53 in 2007, and in 2010, Press 53 will put out his next collection, *Love Chooses You*. In 2009, Sunnyoutside will release his essay collection, *The Agnostic's Prayer*. His essays and stories have appeared in over fifty literary journals and have been cited by *The Best American Short Stories*, *The Best American Mystery Stories*, and *The Best American Spiritual Writing*.

K.H. Solomon is a retired agricultural engineer, whose career specialized in water management. His poems have appeared or are forthcoming in Zyzzyva, *English Journal, River Oak Review, Conclave,* and elsewhere.

Michael Theune's poems, essays, and reviews have appeared in a number of journals, including *The Iowa Review*, *The New Republic*, and *Pleiades*. Additionally, Michael is the editor of *Structure & Surprise: Engaging Poetic Turns* (Teachers & Writers, 2007). He teaches English at Illinois Wesleyan University in Bloomington, Illinois.

Brad Vice is the author of the short story collection *The Bear Bryant Funeral Train*. His fiction has appeared in *The Atlantic Monthly*, *The Georgia Review*, *The Southern Review*, *Shenadoah*, as well as the anthologies *New Stories from the South* and *Best American Voices*. He lives in Pilsen, in the Czech Republic and teaches at the University of West Bohemia.

Susan Woodring is the author of *The Traveling Disease* and *Springtime on Mars: Stories*. Her short fiction can be found in *Isotope, Passages North, Turnrow, The William and Mary Review, Surreal South, Ballyhoo Stories, Quick Fiction* and more. She's also the recipient of the 2006 Elizabeth Simpson Smith Short Fiction Award, the 2006 *Isotope* Editor's Prize, and her story "Inertia" received a notable mention in *Best American Non-Required Reading, 2007*. Susan lives in North Carolina with her family.

Josh Woods won the 2008 Press 53 Open Awards Contest in Genre Fiction, and his stories are published in the *2009 Main Street Rag's Short Fiction Anthology* and in the *Press 53 Open Awards Anthology*. His book review and non-fiction work has been published in *The Susquehanna Review*, *UE Magazine*, and *Crab Orchard Review*. In addition to editing *Versus*, he is also Associate Editor of the upcoming *Surreal South '09* (Press 53). He is currently enrolled in the MFA Fiction Program at Southern Illinois University at Carbondale.